"Absolutely n[o]"

Annie stared at her ex-husband in indignation. Tanner couldn't be suggesting that they go to the *cabin* to write the songs for his next album together. It had been their favorite romantic getaway spot when they were married. They'd spent hours making love in the double bed. Why, she would rather stand in front of a firing squad!

"Why not?" Tanner demanded.

She scowled at him. "Because it's out in the middle of nowhere, and there isn't a nearby motel."

"You don't need to stay at a motel. There's a guest room at the cabin," he challenged.

She met the direct gaze of his blue eyes and felt her heart beat in panic. "If you think I'm going to stay in the same house with you, you're crazy!"

He arched a brow and lowered his voice seductively. "What are you saying, Annie? That you don't trust me? Or that you don't trust yourself?"

Dear Reader,

I'm a genuine romantic. I honestly believe that true love can conquer anything. When I first saw the movie *The Way We Were*, I felt frustrated. I loved the movie, but the ending bothered me. Here were two people so much in love that even a cynic could tell they belonged with each other. Yet they couldn't live together. I spent months rewriting the ending to that movie. I knew that a couple that much in love could always work things out.

Even Cowboys Get the Blues was inspired by a host of divorces I've seen over the years where the husband and wife struggled to fulfill a seemingly impossible dream. But once the dream was achieved, their marriage fell apart. In more than one instance, I realized the divorce resulted not because their love died, but because the struggle had been about their identity as a couple, and they didn't know how to share the dream they'd built together. As in the movie *The Way We Were*, they belonged together, but they couldn't find a common ground to solve their problems.

I hope you enjoy Tanner and Annie's Lost Loves story as much as I enjoyed writing it. They struggled to build a dream, and they succeeded, but they didn't know how to deal with that success. They do, however, belong together, and I hope that by the end they will convince you of what I've always contended: True love *can* conquer anything.

Sincerely,

Carin Rafferty

EVEN COWBOYS
GET THE BLUES
CARIN RAFFERTY

Harlequin Books

TORONTO • NEW YORK • LONDON
AMSTERDAM • PARIS • SYDNEY • HAMBURG
STOCKHOLM • ATHENS • TOKYO • MILAN
MADRID • WARSAW • BUDAPEST • AUCKLAND

If you purchased this book without a cover you should be aware
that this book is stolen property. It was reported as "unsold and
destroyed" to the publisher, and neither the author nor the
publisher has received any payment for this "stripped book."

With love to my sister, Judith Lawson.
Remember the good times!

And in memory of Pooh,
who gave me and my husband twenty and a half years of
love and devotion. We miss you, Pooh!

ISBN 0-373-25605-1

EVEN COWBOYS GET THE BLUES

Copyright © 1994 by Linda Kichline.

All rights reserved. Except for use in any review, the reproduction or
utilization of this work in whole or in part in any form by any electronic,
mechanical or other means, now known or hereafter invented, including
xerography, photocopying and recording, or in any information storage
or retrieval system, is forbidden without the written permission of the
publisher, Harlequin Enterprises Limited, 225 Duncan Mill Road,
Don Mills, Ontario, Canada M3B 3K9.

All characters in this book have no existence outside the imagination of
the author and have no relation whatsoever to anyone bearing the same
name or names. They are not even distantly inspired by any individual
known or unknown to the author, and all incidents are pure invention.

This edition published by arrangement with Harlequin Enterprises B. V.

® and TM are trademarks of the publisher. Trademarks indicated with
® are registered in the United States Patent and Trademark Office, the
Canadian Trade Marks Office and in other countries.

Printed in U.S.A.

1

"YOU CAN'T TRUST COWBOYS," Daniel Harris said as he angrily threw a dart at the dart board hanging on his office wall. He threw another dart. "You can't trust musicians." He threw a third dart with such force that it missed the board and impaled itself in the wall. "And you sure as hell can't trust cowboy musicians!" he concluded.

Muttering a curse, Daniel grabbed the telephone receiver and dialed Tanner Chapel's phone number for the fourth time in fifteen minutes. When he got another busy signal, he slammed the receiver into place and raked a hand through the gray fringe of hair encircling his bald pate. "What in hell is going on, Tanner?"

A journalist from *People* magazine was supposed to have interviewed Tanner at his home this afternoon. She'd called Daniel and informed him that even though Tanner's car was in his driveway, he hadn't answered the door. When she'd driven to a pay phone and tried calling him, the line had been busy. She was livid that the musician stood her up, and Daniel had had a hell of a time pacifying her.

He shook his head in disgust. After nearly thirty years as an agent in the music business, he'd had clients fail to make interviews before. He was surprised, however, that Tanner would pull a stunt like this. The singer was obsessed with his career, and knew how critical this particular article was in promoting his new album. Who was so important that he couldn't ask them to hold while he let the journalist in?

The question nagged at Daniel, because he couldn't think of anyone that significant in Tanner's life. The man's father had deserted him before his birth and his mother had died a few years ago. He didn't have any other family, and his wife, Annie, had divorced him last year. He didn't even have any close friends, because he was so consumed by his career that he had no time to devote to friendships.

Daniel had been ignoring the uneasiness stirring at the back of his mind, but now he acknowledged that if Tanner wasn't talking to someone, it probably meant his phone was off the hook. That worried him. It was so out of character for the musician that Daniel's instincts insisted something must be seriously wrong.

He tried to convince himself that he was overreacting. After all, Tanner was hard at work on songs for his new album. He was probably so engrossed that he'd forgotten about the interview. As for the phone, well, he probably didn't want to be distracted by its ringing, even if the answering machine would pick up calls, so he'd taken it off the hook.

Even though the explanation was plausible, Daniel didn't believe it. With another curse, he hurried out to his car and headed for Tanner's house.

When he arrived, Tanner's car was in the driveway, but no one answered the doorbell. After leaning on it for a good minute, Daniel tried the doorknob. It was locked, so he started around the house, looking for a way in. All the doors and windows on the first floor of the two-story house were also locked. To his frustration, the curtains were closed, so he couldn't even peek inside. By the time he'd gone full circle and was back at the front door, his anxiety had increased tenfold.

He considered calling the police, but quickly dismissed that option. Even if he could persuade them to break in, he didn't know what Tanner was up to inside. The situation could end up generating adverse publicity, and the last thing Tanner needed right now was more bad press. His divorce last year had caused so much hullabaloo that the record company had decided to delay his second album until the furor died down. If there was another delay, it might be the end of Tanner's career, and Daniel couldn't afford to let that happen. He was too close to retirement, and he wanted to spend his golden years basking in luxury, not struggling to make ends meet with a Social Security check and meager savings. Tanner was his last chance to make it big, which meant he had to break into the house.

That would, of course, set off the security system and summon the police, but at least he'd find out what was going on before they got here. It was a hell of a lot easier to perform damage control when you knew beforehand what you were dealing with.

Returning to the backyard, he retrieved a large rock from the border of a flower bed and carried it to the French doors opening into the music room. Raising the rock above his head, he threw it. The window shattered on the first try, and Daniel was surprised when the alarm system didn't begin to blare. What in hell was going on?

With a nervous gulp, he carefully stuck his hand through the broken window, pushed aside the venetian blinds and unlocked the door. When he stepped

into the room, he started to call out to Tanner, but the
cry died on his lips as he stared around him in shock.
The grand piano looked as if an ax had been taken to
it, and indeed, he spied an ax lying nearby. Every piece
of furniture and all the expensive stereo equipment had
been shattered. He spied several holes in the walls, and
when he tried to turn on the overhead light, he discovered that even the light fixtures had been destroyed.

His first thought was that the house had been bur-
glarized, but he'd noticed no evidence of a break-in, and
burglars wouldn't demolish expensive equipment.
Tanner must have done this.

Damn! Daniel should have seen this coming. Ever
since his divorce, the musician had been like a man
possessed. He'd made Daniel book him for appearance
after appearance until the band and road crew had
threatened to walk if they didn't get some time off.
Faced with mutiny, Tanner had finally agreed to a
break, but then he'd had Daniel book him on every
television talk show and charity benefit he could find.

Understanding that work was Tanner's way of cop-
ing with the divorce, the agent had gone along with
him. The way he'd seen it, Tanner was better off
throwing himself into his work than consoling himself
with booze, drugs or women. But when months passed
and he hadn't shown any sign of slowing down, Daniel
had begun to worry that if the singer kept up his frenetic pace, he was going to burn out. Thankfully, the
record company had finally set a date for cutting Tanner's next album, which had given him the perfect excuse to keep Tanner home. He'd figured that once
Tanner began writing songs for his new album, he'd pull

himself together. Another glance around the room confirmed that he'd figured wrong.

He gulped, suddenly realizing that if Tanner had been distraught enough to raze the music room, he might have been crazed enough to harm himself. Urgently he yelled, "Tanner?"

There was no answer, but before he could reach a full-blown panic attack, he heard someone overhead strum chords on a guitar. He hadn't realized he was holding his breath until he released it in a rush. Thank God, Tanner must be okay.

Daniel followed the sound to the master bedroom on the second floor. When he reached the doorway, he saw Tanner sitting against the headboard of the bed, playing his vintage Martin acoustic guitar. All he wore was a pair of torn denims. He had a heavy growth of beard, and his face had the gaunt look of exhaustion. On the bedside table was an ashtray filled with butts, and smoke from a smoldering cigarette curled toward the ceiling.

"What the hell is going on, Tanner?" the agent demanded, stalking to the ashtray to put out the cigarette. "You look like something a cat wouldn't bother to drag in. And you don't smoke."

Still strumming chords, Tanner didn't even look up. "I do now."

"The hell you do," Daniel snapped. "It'll ruin your voice. What are you trying to do? Wreck your career?"

Tanner's head shot up, and the intense fury glowing in his vivid blue eyes made the older man involuntarily take a step back. When Tanner suddenly rose to his knees, raised the guitar over his head and slammed it onto one of the spindle-shaped posts on the bed's footboard, Daniel's mouth dropped open in shock. The guitar was not only worth a fortune, it was Tanner's pride and joy!

Leaving the guitar speared on the post, Tanner sat back on his heels and drawled, "There is no career. It's over."

His comment yanked Daniel out of his stunned state. "Your career isn't over. It's just beginning—that is if you don't blow it by being a jerk," he amended with a scowl. "So stop behaving like some damn prima donna in the throes of a temper tantrum and tell me what's going on here."

"What's going on here is that you were right!" Tanner shot back furiously. "I can't do it without Annie. I can write the music, but I can't write the lyrics. A song doesn't have any meaning without lyrics!"

At his confession, Daniel gave a resigned shake of his head. He'd dreaded that something like this might happen. Though the world thought Tanner wrote all his own music, the truth was that Annie had written the lyrics.

"We talked about this weeks ago," he reminded him. "I told you that since you were used to working as part of a team, you might have trouble writing songs alone. But you don't have to worry about it. I'll find you the best lyricist in the business. You just write the music. I'll take care of the rest."

Tanner almost laughed at the absurdity of Daniel's statement because he knew that the best lyricist in the business wouldn't solve his problem. What Daniel didn't understand—had never understood—was that Annie had been more than his songwriting partner. She'd been his talisman, his lucky charm. She turned his music into magic, and without her magic, he couldn't hold onto the dream.

How could she have deserted him like this? *How could she have walked away from The Dream?*

He felt the panic rising inside him, and no matter how hard he tried, he couldn't keep it at bay. He'd just spent the past month writing the best music he'd ever written, but it didn't mean a damn thing. Annie was the only one who knew him well enough to create words that would give his music his essence. And Annie wasn't here. It was as if his soul was lost in some kind of purgatory and couldn't find its way out.

He was so absorbed in his thoughts that he jumped when Daniel spoke. "Tanner, did you hear me? I said I'll get you the best lyricist in the business, and everything will be okay."

The singer gave a weary shake of his head and bitterly replied, "It isn't going to be okay, because another lyricist can't see inside me the way that Annie can. It *has* to be her or the music won't work."

Daniel rubbed his hand over his bald head. "It has to work without her," he said quietly, "because she's gone and she's not coming back."

"I know," Tanner mumbled. "She's gone and I can't make it without her."

"Look, man, you're exhausted, so you aren't thinking straight. Why don't you get some sleep and then we'll work this out."

Tanner swiveled his head toward his agent and again pinned him with a furious gaze. "Dammit, why won't you listen to me? It won't work without Annie. *It's over!*"

Before Daniel could respond, he bounded off the bed and began to pace. "How could she leave me? How could she just turn her back on all we'd worked toward and walk away? She can't do this to me! *She has to come back and give me the words!*"

As he finished speaking, he stopped in front of the chest of drawers and stared at the cover of his first album, which was hanging over it, framed in glass. Then, he balled his right hand into a fist and aimed at it.

Horrified, Daniel ran to him and grabbed his arm. "Stop it, Tanner! You can't slice your hands to pieces. You need them to work!"

Tanner struggled against his grip, but Daniel was determined to get him under control before he managed to hurt himself. Grabbing his arms, he gave him a hard shake. "Listen to me. I'll find a way to make Annie write the lyrics for you. Do you hear me? *I'll get Annie for you!*"

Tanner stopped struggling and eyed him with wary speculation. "How?"

Daniel shrugged, wondering if he could keep such a rash promise. Annie had made it clear she never wanted to see Tanner again.

"Damned if I know," he admitted with chagrin. "But I swear that if you'll go to bed and get some sleep, I'll find a way to do it. Annie's going to be mad as hell and you sure won't be able to deal with her if you're exhausted."

Frowning, Tanner glanced toward the bed. He was bone weary, but he didn't know if he could sleep. Every time he closed his eyes, the melodies he'd written for the new album kept repeating over and over in his head. They were pulling at him in a way his music never had before, and the fact that he didn't know what they were trying to tell him was driving him insane.

But if Daniel kept his promise, Annie would write the words. Then he'd not only know what the music meant, but it would give him the time he needed to win her back. And to save The Dream.

Wearily he walked to the bed and fell onto the mattress, yawning widely before he said, "You're right. Annie's going to be mad as hell, and I'll have to be at my best in order to handle her. And I can handle her, Daniel. I can."

Daniel didn't bother to respond. He knew that Tanner was trying to convince himself.

After several minutes passed and he was sure Tanner was asleep, he headed back to the music room, where he dug through the chaos until he found the tape deck. As he uncovered it, he arched a brow in surprise. Most of the stereo equipment had been smashed beyond repair, but the tape deck, lying at the bottom of the debris, didn't have a scratch on it. It was almost as if Tanner had gone out of his way to preserve it. Daniel felt the first ray of hope when he pushed the Eject button and the machine opened to reveal a cassette inside.

"Yes!" he declared when he removed it and noted that the tape was on Side B and nearly at the end. He'd been afraid that Tanner hadn't accomplished anything, but it looked like he had. Now he just needed to find out if the music was any good.

He took the tape out to his car, slipped it into the cassette deck and rewound it. Then he crossed his arms over the steering wheel, rested his head against them and prayed as the tape began to play.

By the time it was finished, Daniel was sagging against the car seat in relief. His prayers had been answered. Tanner had written some of the best music he'd heard in years, and dollar signs began to proliferate in his head.

But before they could get the dollars, they had to get the lyrics, he reminded himself. The question was, how could he get Annie to write them? And he was determined to get her, because he was now convinced Tanner was right. No one but Annie could do proper justice to this music. She was a gifted writer and she knew Tanner's style. Daniel had always felt that it was just a matter of time before she was touted as one of the best lyricists in the business. He was also sure that if she wrote the lyrics to this music, they'd have so many hits they'd all be rich.

Rubbing his hands together in anticipation, the agent went back into the house and got the telephone in working order. Then he sat down in a chair in the living room and settled the phone on his knees. There was only one person who could solve this dilemma, and that was Roy Wilson, the chief executive officer of New Country Records. NCR produced Tanner's albums, and Annie was one of their contract lyricists. If Roy told her she had to work with Tanner, she'd have no other choice.

As he dialed Roy's number, Daniel felt a flash of guilt. He'd always liked Annie, and he didn't blame her for divorcing Tanner. In her place, he'd have divorced him, too. Forcing her to work with him was not only cruel, it was unconscionable.

But when the phone began to ring, he shrugged away the guilt. Only a fool let his conscience interfere with business, and this wasn't just business for him. Those golden years were getting too close for comfort. If he had to sacrifice Annie to keep Tanner on top and ensure his own future, so be it. She was young, and unlike him, she had plenty of time to bounce back.

When Roy's secretary answered, he crossed his fingers and mentally beseeched, *Oh, God, please let me pull this off!*

ANNIE O'NEILL-CHAPEL plunked her elbows onto the piano keys, buried her face in her hands and heaved a discouraged sigh. For the past week she'd been trying to write the lyrics to a melody, and she still hadn't come up with a theme, let alone a single word. The most frustrating part was that it was a light, fun tune that made you want to tap your feet and clap your hands. Normally, this was the type of music that inspired her and she was able to whip out the lyrics in a matter of hours. But during the past few months the music hadn't been "speaking" to her like it used to, and that worried her. She was afraid she was losing her touch.

The thought caused a panic to stir inside her. Before the emotion could overwhelm her, she sat up straight and impatiently shook her head.

"Just because you're experiencing a little creative block doesn't mean you're washed up," she scolded herself. "This happens to artists all the time, and the only way to get through it is to keep working until something clicks."

An hour later, however, she still hadn't made any progress. Agitated, she rose and walked to the window of her second-story apartment. As she stared out at the concrete parking lot and the bland, redbrick apart-

ment complex on the other side, she felt the panic rising again.

Wrapping her arms around her middle, she struggled against the sudden churning in her stomach. What
would she do if she could no longer write lyrics?

She wasn't worried about making a living. After
working for several years as a waitress and a part-time
salesclerk to support herself and Tanner while he pur-
sued his dream of becoming a star, she'd decided to get
an education in a field that would guarantee her a well-
paying job. A couple of years before Tanner landed his
recording contract, she'd started taking college night
courses in accounting. She'd stopped going to school
when Tanner's dream finally came true, but she was
only a few semesters away from getting her degree. She
could easily go back, finish her education and get a lu-
crative job.

But writing words to songs wasn't a job for her; it was
a compulsion. She was painfully shy. Outside of her
family, Tanner was the only person she'd felt comfortable enough with to reveal her innermost feelings.
That's why writing lyrics was so important. Through
them she was able to release the emotions she was unable to verbalize otherwise. And since her divorce, she
had an excess of emotions that had to be let out, she
grimly admitted. So why, when it was so critical to her
well-being, was her Muse deserting her? What *would*
she do if she could no longer write lyrics?

She was startled out of her troubled reverie by the
sound of the doorbell. A glance toward the clock indicated it was shortly after noon, which meant it was
probably her older sister, Lisa, dropping by during her
lunch hour.

Annie's first impulse was to ignore the bell. Her mood was too morose for her to handle even her big sister's company. But then she remembered that Roy Wilson was sending her a demo tape by courier. He'd instructed her to listen to the tape immediately and let him know if she wanted to take on the project.

As she headed for the door, she nervously rubbed her hands against her thighs. When Roy had called that morning, she'd been surprised. The CEO of NCR rarely got involved in the creative end of the business, which meant this tape must belong to either a big-name star or a new composer in whom he'd taken a special interest.

That he'd chosen her to work on the project should have thrilled her, but she was terrified. If she accepted the assignment and couldn't write the lyrics, her career would be destroyed. Then again, if she turned it down, Roy would want to know why. Telling him the truth might also destroy her career. She was in the proverbial no-win situation.

She opened the door with trepidation, to find the courier standing there. After he left, she tore open the envelope and studied the cassette. Beside Roy's name there was nothing on the label, which she found odd. Normally demo tapes listed the name of the composer, a brief description of the music and the date it had been recorded. Did that mean it was a big-name star? No, she quickly decided. It had to be an unknown. No stars would let their original music leave their possession without their name on it.

Recognizing that she was putting off the inevitable, she reluctantly walked to the tape deck and popped in the cassette. Then she grabbed the remote control, crossed to the sofa and sat down. After hitting the Play button, she leaned back against the cushions and closed her eyes, letting the opening strains of the first melody wash over her. The music was filled with so much heartbreak that it brought tears to her eyes, and within moments she was spellbound.

The emotions it evoked were soul wrenching, and she grabbed a nearby throw pillow and crushed it to her chest as tears began to run unchecked down her cheeks. As impossible as it seemed, the next melody was as lamentable as the first, and even more heartbreakingly beautiful. She felt as if the composer was delving inside her and suffering her heartbreak over Tanner along with her. How, after all this time, could there still be so much pain?

By the time she had listened to the half-dozen melodies, she felt as if the composer had turned her inside out, leaving her emotionally raw and vulnerably exposed. With a ragged sigh, she wiped away her tears and stared at the tape deck in awe. The music had been sorrowful, but it had also been cathartic, because her creative block was gone. Her mind was literally teeming with ideas for every one of the magnificent melodies.

She wanted to run to the window, throw it open and scream her joy to the world. She compromised by grabbing the telephone receiver and dialing Roy's office. When he came on the line, she said, "I want this assignment, Roy. No, I *demand* to have it."

He chuckled. "Does this mean you like the music?"

"Like it?" she repeated with a laugh. "I don't *like* it. I *love* it! We're talking masterpieces. Who's the genius who wrote this music, and when can I meet him or her?"

"How about ten tomorrow in my office?" he suggested.

"I'll be there."

It wasn't until she hung up that she realized Roy hadn't told her the composer's name. She considered calling him back, but decided it wasn't worth bothering him just to satisfy her curiosity. Besides, she was sure it was some new talent, so the name wouldn't mean anything to her.

She contented herself by rewinding the tape and losing herself in the music again. Amazingly, it was even more beautiful on the second playing. For the first time in months, she was eager to get to work.

"Whoever you are, thank you from the bottom of my heart!" she declared, hurrying to the piano. Before she could start on the new project, she had to write the song she'd been agonizing over all week.

As she slid onto the piano bench, she suddenly knew exactly what words to use. She should be done in a couple of hours, and then she could start developing her ideas for the music on the demo.

2

"ANNIE, IT'S SO GOOD to see you!" Roy declared. He rose from his mahogany-and-leather executive chair, so large and ornate it resembled a throne, and gestured toward one of the plush, red leather chairs sitting in front of his desk. "Please, come in and have a seat."

"It's good to see you, too, Roy," Annie responded as she walked to the chair. When she sat down, she nervously glanced around the room. She'd been in this office only once before—the day Roy had signed Tanner to a recording contract.

A strong sense of déjà vu rushed through her as she recalled that the last time she'd been here the sun had been shining through the floor-to-ceiling windows overlooking downtown Nashville just as it was today. Roy had been sitting behind his gigantic mahogany desk just as he was now. She'd been seated in the same spot in front of his desk. But there the similarities ended.

During her last visit, there had been only a half-dozen awards on display, but now every available space was cluttered with them. One of the awards was due to Tanner's and her efforts. Only a handful of people knew that, however. She'd insisted that Tanner copyright their songs in his name alone. Fool that she was, she'd felt that he might have a better chance of making it if people thought he'd written the songs in their entirety.

She'd figured that, since they were married, it didn't matter if her name was on the copyright. All the money would go into one account anyway. It had been a selfless, wifely act that had turned out to be a foolish mistake.

Thankfully, Roy had known the truth and offered her a job as a contract lyricist when she'd filed for divorce. With any luck, this project would prove to him that his faith in her was justified.

Returning her gaze to her employer, she asked, "So where's the musical genius I'm supposed to meet? I've already come up with some ideas on the melodies, and I can't wait to discuss them."

"He'll be here shortly. I wanted to talk to you before you met with him."

It wasn't Roy's words but something elusive in his tone that made Annie regard him warily. "Is something wrong?"

"Not as far as I'm concerned."

Again it wasn't his words but his tone that disturbed her. Something was going on, and she suspected she knew what it was. There was a lot of competition among the contract lyricists, and she was the new kid on the block. Many of them would resent Roy singling her out for his pet project. They might try to convince him that she was too inexperienced for this job.

Just the thought that she might not be able to write the lyrics for this music made Annie's stomach clench. Hearing the tape had broken her creative block, but would that block come back if the project was taken away from her?

She tried to tell herself that she was being silly. After all, Roy had just said there was nothing wrong. She knew, however, that it was exactly that head-in-the-sand attitude that had made her look like a fool when the truth about Tanner had come out. After that experience, she'd vowed that she would never again ignore her instincts. She might be shy, but, thanks to Tanner, she'd learned the hard way that it was better to confront an uncomfortable situation than to have it blow up in your face.

Drawing in a fortifying breath, she asked, "Roy, is someone upset that you've given me this project?"

He blinked, as if truly startled by her question. "No."

She frowned in confusion. "Then what's the problem? And don't tell me there isn't one. I can hear it in your voice."

Roy leaned back in his chair and eyed her thoughtfully. "As far as I'm concerned there isn't a problem, but you may feel differently." He swiveled his chair toward the windows and then swung back to face her. "Annie, Tanner is the composer."

Annie was so dumbfounded that she shook her head, sure she'd misunderstood him. But no matter how much she wanted to deny it, his grim expression assured her that that was exactly what he was saying. She glanced around the room, trying to come to grips with this turn of events.

Again, the memory of the last time she'd been in this office surfaced. In her mind, she saw Roy toast Tanner and her with champagne after Tanner signed his contract. She could actually hear the sound of crystal as she and Tanner clinked their glasses together and grinned at each other. She even experienced the elation she'd felt knowing that after all their hard work, Tanner's dream of becoming a star was finally coming true.

Unfortunately, as she'd indulged in the excitement of that moment, she hadn't known that Tanner had already killed the dream for her. It would be another year and a half before she'd discover his betrayal and her world would fall apart.

Unable to bear the pain of what might have been—no, what *should* have been—she lowered her gaze to the thick gray carpet.

Tanner had written that beautiful, soul-wrenching music. He'd been the one to make her feel as if he'd delved inside her and suffered her heartbreak right along with her, and she knew that wasn't true. Damn him, damn him, damn him, damn him!

"Annie, are you okay?"

Roy's question pulled her out of her mental litany. When she glanced up at him, her temper flared. Normally, she would have remained quiet—kept all that anger bottled up inside—but this time she felt her emotions break free. Besides, if her feelings couldn't be released through rage, she knew she would burst into tears, and she couldn't embarrass herself in front of Roy by crying over a rat like Tanner Thaddeus Chapel.

"No, I'm not fine, and I can't believe you'd pull a stunt like this on me," she replied, keeping her tone even. She might be furious, but she wasn't so out of control that she would lose her professionalism. "There is no way I can work with Tanner."

Roy, who with his short, stout body, warm brown eyes and silver-gray hair resembled a benevolent grandfather, studied her intently. His scrutiny made Annie so nervous that she had to fight to keep from squirming in her chair. She was well aware that though he looked benevolent, he was known for his ruthlessness. He also had enough power to make or break a career in Nashville, and he was notorious for getting what he wanted. Right now he wanted her to work with Tanner.

Suddenly, she felt sick to her stomach. If it had been anyone else, she could have handled the situation by telling Roy to just let her work from the tape. She could have sent drafts back and forth to the musician until she came up with lyrics that he or she liked. However, when Tanner had been offered a contract, she'd insisted that he make sure he had a clause in it not only guaranteeing him complete artistic control over his music, but ensuring that he participate personally in writing the lyrics. It had been a totally selfish suggestion on her part, because she'd wanted to continue as his lyricist. She'd been afraid that the record company might make him use one of theirs, thus cutting her out of the creative process.

"Why can't you work with him?" Roy finally asked, pulling her away from her memories. "Are you still in love with him?"

"Of course I'm not in love with him!" she exclaimed. "But Tanner and I are divorced, and at the risk of sounding trite, if I never see him again it would be too soon."

He gave a solemn nod. "I know that your divorce wasn't amicable, Annie, which is why I didn't tell you the demo was Tanner's. I wanted your professional response to the music, not a prejudiced one, and you reacted just as I thought you would. You fell in love with it."

Annie wanted to tell him that she hated Tanner's music, but it was too late for that. *Damn!* She always did this. When was she going to learn to keep her mouth shut until she knew all the important facts?

"I do love the music," she admitted grudgingly. "But I still can't work with Tanner, and if you had been honest with me, we wouldn't be wasting our time on this conversation."

He leaned his elbows on the arms of his chair and propped his hands in a steeple beneath his chin. "Maybe I should have been honest with you, but I also think you need to be honest with yourself. On some level you had to know the music was Tanner's. You two were together too long for you not to recognize his style. I can only assume that the creative side of your nature stopped you from acknowledging the work as his because you wanted to write the lyrics, even if it meant you'd have to work with him."

"If I wanted to be psychoanalyzed, I'd go to a professional counselor," Annie retorted, crossing her legs and swinging her foot in an angry cadence. Why hadn't she recognized the music as Tanner's? Because it was so different from anything he'd ever composed, the possibility had never occurred to her. Yet, as some of the melodies began to play in her head, she realized that his inimitable style was subtly woven throughout the music. She *should* have realized it was his. That she hadn't infuriated her.

"I'm not trying to psychoanalyze you, Annie. I'm merely pointing out the obvious."

"Well, you can point out anything you want, but that doesn't change the fact that I cannot—I *will* not—work with Tanner," she amended. "When you said our divorce wasn't amicable, you made the understatement of the century. He turned the entire humiliating mess into a three-ring circus. For pity's sake, he even filed for custody of my cat, and he hates my cat!"

Roy nodded again. "I do understand how you feel, Annie, but considering your avid response to Tanner's music, I'm convinced that you and he are a perfect creative match."

At his words, Annie felt panic rising inside her. She *couldn't* work with Tanner, and somehow she had to convince Roy of that.

"We did make a good team," she said, leaning forward in her chair to add emphasis to her words. "But you know as well as I do that there are a dozen fantastic, not to mention well-known, lyricists out there who would kill to write the lyrics to Tanner's music."

"You're right," he agreed, "and ordinarily, I'd let you off the hook. The problem is, Tanner's scheduled to record his new album in six weeks. There just isn't time to find another compatible lyricist to work with him."

"So delay the album," Annie suggested.

"I can't, or more accurately, won't do that." He, too, leaned forward, folding his arms on top of his desk. "Tanner's first album almost reached number one, and I'm going to do everything in my power to make sure that his second album does exactly that. That's why I want it out in time for the Christmas season. In order to meet that goal, I have no alternative but to give you this assignment."

"And if I refuse to accept it?"

He gave a negligent shrug and sank back in his chair. "You'll be in breach of contract, which means I'll be forced to take legal action against you. It could be *years* before we settle the matter, and until it is settled, you wouldn't be able to work anywhere in the music industry."

Annie stared at him, aghast. She knew he was ruthless, but she would have never believed he'd resort to outright blackmail. "You're threatening me!"

"I sure am," he admitted without batting an eye. "But look at this from my standpoint. It's my job to do whatever it takes to get Tanner to the top of the charts, and this move can only help your own career. You and Tanner have already won a Grammy for your work together, even if no one else knows you wrote the lyrics. There's no reason why you can't win more with this album, and this time you'll get the credit you deserve.

"You should also consider that your contract with us expires next year," he went on. "If you have an award or two under your belt, you won't have to work under contract. You'll be in such demand that you can freelance, which means you'll be in a position to tell people like me to go to hell."

"That last possibility is almost enough incentive for me to go along with you," Annie stated dryly. "But even if I did, Tanner isn't going to agree with this. He was furious with me for divorcing him, and believe me, when he's mad, he stays mad. I doubt he can be civil to me, let alone work with me."

"Well, there's only one way to find out," he said, glancing at his watch and rising. "Tanner should be waiting outside. I'll send him in and the two of you can talk while I take a coffee break."

Annie felt the color draining from her face. It was one thing to discuss Tanner. It was an entirely different matter to meet him face-to-face, particularly when she hadn't had time to prepare for such a scene. Then again, if Roy gave her a hundred years, she wouldn't be prepared. This was one of her worst nightmares come to life!

"You want me to meet with Tanner *now*?" she asked, hating the quaver in her voice but unable to stop it.

"We're on a short deadline, Annie. The faster you and Tanner clear the air, the faster the two of you can get to work."

Annie started to object, but before she could open her mouth Roy walked out of the office, closing the door behind him.

She frantically glanced around the room for a means of escape, even though she knew that the only other way out was an eight-story swan dive from the plate-glass windows.

Closing her eyes, she gave a resigned shake of her head. She was trapped, and in just a few minutes, Tanner would be closing in for the kill.

As TANNER WAITED for Roy to summon him to his office, he could barely keep from pacing. If it hadn't been for the secretary eyeing him with covert curiosity, he might have succumbed to the urge. But he wasn't about to let anyone—not even Roy's secretary—know how nervous he was.

Sitting down on the overstuffed, white leather sofa, he propped his booted feet atop some magazines on the glass coffee table. Then he pulled the brim of his Stetson down over his eyes and crossed his arms on his chest, pretending to doze while trying to imagine what was happening between Roy and Annie. He knew that Roy thought it would be easy to persuade her to work with him. The executive had pointed out that she'd not only fallen in love with his music, but she'd called him a musical genius. Roy also claimed that Annie was a consummate professional and would never let her personal feelings stand in the way of her career.

Tanner was willing to allow that, under normal circumstances, Annie would never let her personal feelings get in the way of business. Unfortunately, these were not normal circumstances, and he had bet Roy twenty bucks that the CEO would have to threaten her to get her to write the lyrics to his music. Even then Tanner wasn't sure she'd do it. The one thing he'd learned during their marriage was that she was as unpredictable as the weather and twice as contrary. It would be just like her to walk away from her career so she wouldn't have to work with him.

But that wasn't going to happen, he assured himself. Roy would persuade her to take on the project, and then Tanner could put his own plan into action. Annie belonged by his side, and by the time the songs were written, he was going to have proved that to her. They'd remarry, be the songwriting team they'd always been, and The Dream they'd built together would never die.

As he made the assertion, a nagging inner voice told him he was being overconfident. He hadn't believed Annie would divorce him, but she had. What made him so sure he could win her back?

Even though doubt began to assail him, he refused to let it surface. When Daniel had promised him he'd get Annie to write the lyrics to his songs, Tanner had told himself that all he had to do was believe that they'd get back together and it would happen. As long as he didn't panic, he could *make* it happen. He just had to stay in control and everything would be all right. It *had* to be all right.

His thoughts were interrupted by the sound of Roy's office door opening and closing. He wanted to leap to his feet and demand to know what had happened. Instead, he nonchalantly pushed up his hat brim, stretched and faked a yawn before drawling, "Morning, Roy. How's it going?"

Roy ignored him as he turned to his secretary and said, "Ellen, you can take your break now."

The woman arched a brow at the dismissal, but retrieved her purse from her desk and left without a word. When she was gone, Roy turned to face Tanner, scowling as he dug a twenty-dollar bill out of his pocket.

When he extended the money, Tanner realized that he'd won the bet. Roy had had to threaten Annie, and even though Tanner had anticipated it, it irritated the hell out of him. How could she call him a musical genius and then refuse to work with him?

"How mad is she?" he asked as he took the bill and stuffed it into his shirt pocket.

"On a scale of one to ten, I'd say about twelve," Roy muttered, plopping down on the sofa Tanner had just vacated. He scowled again. "I hope you realize that you've just cost me one of the best lyricists in the business. After this, she'll never renew her contract, so you'd better not blow it, Tanner."

"I have no intention of blowing this," Tanner responded irritably. "We are, after all, talking about my career."

Roy nodded. "Yes, we are, so get in there and do whatever it takes to make peace with her. You have only six weeks to get those songs written."

Tanner shoved a hand into his pants pocket and strolled toward the door. "Don't worry, Roy. I know how to handle Annie. When you walk back into your office, the air will be filled with white doves bearing olive branches."

"To hell with the doves," Roy grumbled. "When I walk back in there I want to see a smile on Annie's face."

Tanner grasped the doorknob and glanced over his shoulder, grimly noting, "I'd like to see her smile, too, Roy. But I promised to make peace with her today, not perform a miracle."

"Well, something tells me you're going to have to do both."

ANNIE HAD BEEN anticipating Tanner's arrival, but when he walked in, she silently thanked the heavens that she was still sitting. Otherwise she was sure her knees would have buckled from the nervous tremor that shot through her.

Her gaze automatically flicked from the black Stetson that topped his shaggy, dark blond hair to his black leather cowboy boots. He was wearing a Western-style chambray shirt that stretched across his broad shoulders and emphasized the narrowness of his waist. His faded denims hung seductively low on his narrow hips and fit him so intimately that her mind instantly conjured up a number of X-rated memories.

She inwardly cursed both the memories and the hot tickle of desire that slithered deep inside her. She despised Tanner, so how could he still have this kind of an effect on her?

For the same reason that he tickles millions of women all over the world. He's got animal magnetism, and he knows exactly how to use it.

Fearing that he might pick up on her wayward thoughts, she quickly shifted her gaze to his face. It looked thinner than she remembered, and the faint lines bracketing his startling blue eyes and his perfectly sculpted mouth were a bit deeper. To her vexation, the changes enhanced rather than detracted from his rugged handsomeness. After all he'd put her through, the least he could have done was look a little ragged around the edges.

But to look ragged, he would have had to suffer, and he hadn't suffered, she grimly reminded herself. He'd merely thrown a temper tantrum because she'd had the gall to walk out on him before he'd had the opportunity to walk out on her. And his leaving would have been inevitable, she knew. He was too dynamic to be stuck with a shy, ordinary woman like herself for the rest of his life.

A tangle of emotions—bitterness, hurt and, oddly enough, regret—swept over her at that admission. Before she could sort through them, he closed the door, leaned against it and crossed his arms over his chest. Then he flashed her a smile.

Annie regarded him warily. She'd met Tanner when she was sixteen and he was eighteen, had married him when she was eighteen and he was twenty. They'd lived together for ten years, and she'd learned long ago that he was at his most dangerous when he was smiling. And the more teeth he showed, the more dangerous he was. Right now he could have been on a poster for a dental-hygiene advertisement, and she suddenly understood what was going on here.

The day their divorce became final, he'd told her that he'd get even with her. What better way to achieve that goal than to destroy her career? And Roy had made it clear that that was exactly what would happen if she refused to work on this project. She was sure Tanner was counting on her to do just that.

She wanted to rail at him, but, thankfully, her pride surfaced before she could succumb to the urge. Yelling wouldn't change anything, because he held the winning hand. He was the star. She was nothing more than a lyricist who could be replaced.

Raising her chin a notch, she glared at him. He might think he'd defeated her, but she'd be damned if she went down without a fight.

Tanner thought he'd been prepared to see Annie, but when he walked into the room and his gaze settled on her sweet, heart-shaped face, he was so overcome with emotion he could barely breathe. He knew he'd missed her, but until now he hadn't realized how much.

As he took in her form-fitting, navy blue business suit and wraparound, white silk blouse, he wanted to rush across the room and haul her slender body into his arms. He wanted to bury his fingers in her soft, shoulder-length fall of russet hair and gaze deeply into her dark brown eyes, to prove to himself it was really her. However, her belligerent expression assured him that such an act would be dangerous, so he suppressed the impulse.

As he continued to stare at her, he knew he should say something. He was afraid, however, that if he opened his mouth, he'd start yelling at her for putting him through this unnecessary past year and a half of hell. Yes, he had made a mistake. A bad mistake. But after all they'd been through together, she hadn't even considered giving him a second chance. Instead she'd hightailed it to the nearest divorce attorney. *Dammit!* She hadn't even given him the opportunity to explain what had happened.

All the old frustration began to rise inside him, but he forced it back down and promised himself that no matter what happened, he was not going to lose his temper. Besides, he was not here to rehash the past. He was here to secure his future and his career, and the first step in accomplishing that goal was to make peace with her.

Unfortunately, the glare she had fixed on him guaranteed that that was not going to be an easy feat, but what else was new? Nothing involving Annie was ever easy. It was an aspect of her personality that had driven him crazy. Oddly enough, it was also one of the things about her he'd missed the most.

Forcing himself to give her his widest, friendliest smile, he said, "Hello, Annie. How are you?"

The moment the words left his mouth, he knew it was the wrong question to ask. When she shot to her feet, her eyes flashing and her hair bristling, he realized that Roy was right. If he hoped to pull this off, he was going have to come up with a miracle—and fast!

3

"YOU WANT TO KNOW how I *am*?" Annie gasped in outrage as she jumped to her feet, put her hands on her hips and glared at Tanner. "Fine. I'll tell you how I am. I shouldn't have divorced you. I should have run you over with my car half a dozen times to make sure I got you out of my life for good! Unfortunately, you're probably like that guy in those horror movies—the ones where they keep killing him off at the end, but he keeps coming back for another sequel."

Tanner let out an exasperated sigh. "Annie, you're overreacting, as usual."

"*Overreacting?*" she repeated with an angry toss of her head. "You are the most despicable man I've ever met, Tanner Chapel. After everything you've done to me, I can't believe you're being this petty. Wasn't it enough that you had to humiliate me in front of the entire world? Do you also have to take away my career? Do you hate me that much?"

Tanner felt his defenses rise at her unwarranted attack, but he reminded himself that he was supposed to make peace with her. He vented his frustration by tapping the toe of his boot against the floor. "I don't hate you, Annie, and if you're implying that I'm trying to carry out some vendetta against you, you're wrong."

"And, of course, you expect me to believe that," she snapped, spinning on her heel and stalking to the windows.

As she stared out the glass, he said, "Yes, I do expect you to believe that, because it's true."

"Sure. And I'm Johnny Cash."

"Dammit, Annie! You're starting to test my patience."

"Oh, well, please forgive me!" She turned to face him and affected a perfect Scarlett O'Hara simper. "Just because my ex-husband is a low-down, dirty, rotten rat, I shouldn't be so uncouth as to test his patience. I don't know what came over me. My mother taught me better manners than that. Perhaps I should buzz Roy's secretary and ask her to bring in a pot of tea. I'm sure that will soothe your frazzled nerves."

Tanner ground his teeth. He'd forgotten how sarcastic she could be when she was angry. "Will you just answer a simple question for me?" he managed calmly, albeit with extraordinary effort.

"I suppose that depends on what the question is," she answered, eyeing him suspiciously.

"Do you like the music I've composed?"

She turned back to face the windows. "It's . . . nice."

"Why, Annie, I'm humbled to receive such high praise from you," he muttered dryly.

She gave a resigned shrug. "Okay, Tanner. It's better than nice. I think it's the best music you've ever written, but . . ."

"But you don't want to work with me," he finished. When she didn't respond, he said, "I guess I don't blame you. If I was in your place, I wouldn't want to work with me, either."

"Then why are you asking me to?"

"Because I think you're the best lyricist in the business, and I'd be a fool not to want the best. I was hoping that if we sat down and talked, I could persuade you to put your personal feelings aside and work with me on a professional basis."

She let out a brittle laugh. "You know, Tanner, I'd forgotten what a superb manipulator you are. You want to lull me into complacency, and then when I least expect it, you'll stick in the knife and give it a few good twists, right?"

Before he could respond, she went on, "Well, your plan isn't going to work, because I'm no longer the guileless, gullible woman you married. I know what you're up to. You want me to turn down this assignment, and then Roy will fire me and I'll never work in Nashville again. But your plan just backfired on you, because if you think you can destroy me that easily, you're in for one heck of a surprise. I'm not going to walk away from you. I'm going to write the lyrics to your damn melodies, and I'm going to turn every one of them into hits. Then, when I'm standing there with an armful of Grammies, I'm going to tell both you and Roy to go straight to hell. After that, I'll go into business for myself and devote my entire life to writing lyrics for other people's songs—songs that will knock you right off the charts. So what do you think about that?"

"I think that if anyone can carry out that threat, it's you," he answered. Tanner knew better than to argue with success, even if he wasn't sure how he'd just achieved it. Though she'd vowed to wreck his career, he wasn't particularly worried about that. If everything went according to plan—and he had every inten-

tion of ensuring that it did—she'd be his wife again by
the time the songs were completed. "Do you have anything else to say?"

"No," she answered sullenly.

"Okay. Let me see if I've got this straight. You're going to write the lyrics for my new album, win me tons
of awards, tell Roy and me to go to hell and then go into
business for yourself to make sure I never have a hit
record again. Have I overlooked anything, or have we
got a deal?"

Annie regarded him suspiciously. He should have
been furious that she'd thwarted his plan, but he was
grinning at her! Just what was he up to? The only log-
ical answer was that he wanted her to accept the project so he could sabotage her at every turn until Roy was
forced to fire her for incompetence. Then she really
would never be able to work in Nashville again and his
revenge would be complete.

She crossed her arms over her chest in a mimicry of
his own stance and gave him her best haughty look. She
hadn't been kidding when she'd said he wouldn't destroy her that easily, and he really was going to be in for
a big surprise. When she'd been married to him, she'd
had about as much backbone as a kitten. Since the divorce, however, she'd not only grown some claws, she
was looking forward to using them on him.

"We have a deal."

"I KNEW THAT IF THE TWO of you sat down and talked,
you could work things out," Roy stated smugly as he
settled behind his desk.

"Yeah, Roy. You missed your calling. You should have
gone into family counseling. I'm sure that blackmail

and threats are a technique no one has considered before," Annie muttered.

He pointedly ignored her sarcasm as he turned his attention to Tanner. "So, when are you going to get to work?"

"I suppose that depends on when you can book us some studio time," Annie replied before Tanner could answer. The alternative was to work at the house they'd bought together, and she simply couldn't handle that.

"Studio time?" Roy shook his head. "All the studios are booked for the next month, and even if they weren't, I don't want you working here. The press will pick up on Tanner's presence, and we'll have every fan and tourist in town waiting outside to catch a glimpse of him. That would be a security nightmare. No, it would be better if you worked at Tanner's house."

Tanner felt himself pale as he recalled the state of the music room. There was no way he could let Annie see what he'd done to it. One look and she'd realize how desperate he was. That was too dangerous a weapon for her to have, particularly when she was intent on ruining him.

"We can't work at the house, Roy. I'm having some, um, remodeling done and the noise is horrendous," he said, improvising quickly. "Maybe we can work at Annie's place."

"No way!" Annie exclaimed, ignoring the gut-twisting sensation brought on by the knowledge that Tanner was remodeling her house—no, *his* house. "I live in an apartment building. If we're working day and night, my neighbors will have me evicted."

Roy gave them an impatient frown. "Well, you're going to have to work somewhere. Do either of you have any suggestions?"

"Not a one," Annie answered, shooting a triumphant look toward Tanner. "Maybe someone is trying to tell us something, like this partnership isn't meant to be."

Tanner regarded her through narrowed eyes. It was obvious she was looking for a way to renege on their deal, and he knew she'd continue to do so until she succeeded. That meant he needed to get her somewhere secluded, so she wouldn't have an opportunity to escape. Now that he had her back in his grasp, he wasn't about to let her get away.

Suddenly, the perfect solution came to him. There was one place that had everything they needed to work, plus it was where they'd honeymooned. With all those memories, it was the perfect spot for him to woo her back to his side where she belonged.

Flashing her a smile, he drawled, "I agree that someone's trying to tell us something, Annie, but it isn't that our partnership isn't meant to be. It's that if we hope to get these songs written in time, we'll need isolation. There's only one place I can think of that's quiet, isolated and has all the equipment we need. The cabin."

Annie stared at him in horror. He couldn't be suggesting that they go to *the* cabin. Why, she'd rather stand in front of a firing squad!

"Absolutely not!"

"Why not?" Tanner demanded.

She scowled at him. "Because it's out in the middle of nowhere, and there isn't a nearby motel."

"You don't need to stay at a motel. There's a guest room at the cabin."

"If you think I'm going to stay in the same house with you, you're crazy!"

He raised one eyebrow and lowered his voice seductively. "What are you saying, Annie? That you don't trust me? Or maybe it's that you don't trust yourself."

The sexy timbre of his voice sent a wicked shiver skittering down her spine. She cursed her body for its traitorous reaction to such an obvious ploy.

"I trust myself just fine. It's you I don't trust," she retorted. "And as you well know, I have every reason not to."

Her jab hit its mark, and despite his resolve to hold onto his temper, Tanner snapped, "Dammit, Annie! That's your problem. A guy makes one mistake and you can't forgive him for it!"

Her expression turned murderous. "Your one mistake is every woman's worst nightmare!"

"Time-out!" Roy bellowed. When Annie and Tanner jerked their heads toward him, he glowered at them. "Look, I know you two have some personal problems, but quite frankly, all I care about is getting an album recorded. That isn't going to happen unless you stop bickering and get some songs written. So how about if you put your private grievances aside and start acting like professionals?"

"You're right, Roy." Tanner quickly recovered his composure. "We need to act like professionals, and that's why I think we should go to the cabin. If we're going to meet our deadline, we need seclusion so we can concentrate on our work. The cabin will give us that."

"Annie, do you think you can work at the cabin?" Roy asked.

Annie refused to look at him, because she didn't want him to see the tears burning her eyes. Tanner couldn't have picked a more perfect way to torment her. She was tempted to tell both of them to go jump in the nearest lake, but she knew that if she did, Roy would fire her.

She took a moment to get her roiling emotions under control and then said, "I'm willing to try it for a week, Roy. If during that time Tanner proves that he can behave professionally toward me, I'll consider staying if it's necessary. With the notes I have, and if we work hard, I think we could complete the songs in a week. However, at the first sign of unprofessionalism from Tanner, regardless of whether the songs are done, I'm walking."

"Yeah, well, you're really good at that, aren't you?" Tanner muttered.

"Just what does that mean?" she demanded, frowning at him.

"Walking," he said, frowning back at her. "You're not committing to this business arrangement any more than you did to our marriage. If something goes wrong, then you'll be gone without a backward glance."

Annie was so flabbergasted by his accusation that for a moment she couldn't even find the words to rebut it. But her astonishment was quickly replaced with anger. "How dare you accuse me of a lack of commitment to our marriage! You're the one who not only had an affair, but was irresponsible enough to father a child during it!"

Tanner bolted upright in his chair, so angered by her charges that his entire body began to tremble. "You're quoting the damn tabloids without even knowing the full story. But, of course, you're going to read them before you listen to me, right? I mean, after all, they are *so* reputable and they *always* get their facts straight."

"Well, in your case, they got them right, didn't they?"

"Enough!" Roy yelled. When they again jerked their heads toward him, he said, "This is a place of business, and I expect you both to behave like mature adults. Now, Annie, will you work at the cabin?"

Annie wanted to give him an emphatic no, but one look at Tanner's face assured her that that was what he expected her to say. She wasn't about to live up to any of his expectations, even if it did mean she'd have to go to the cabin.

"I already said I'd give it a week to see if Tanner can treat me like a professional."

"Then it's settled," Roy said, thumping a fist on his desk. "But I'm warning you, Tanner. If you behave unprofessionally toward Annie, she has my permission to leave, and I will never ask her to work with you again. Got that?"

"Yeah, I've got it," Tanner grumbled. "My only question is, who determines if my behavior is unprofessional?"

"Are you insinuating that I'd accuse you falsely?" Annie asked.

He leveled a stony gaze at her. "It wouldn't be the first time, would it? Besides, you don't trust me, so why should I trust you?"

Before Annie could come up with a scathing-enough response, Roy said, "I'll be the one who decides who is being unprofessional. Do either of you have a problem with that?"

Actually, Annie had a big problem with that. Tanner was the star, and Roy, by his own admission, was willing to do whatever it took to make sure he stayed that way. Tanner would probably have to murder her and bury her in the backyard before Roy would consider his actions unprofessional.

But even as she opened her mouth to object, she again recognized that by doing so, she'd be acting as Tanner expected. "That's fine with me, Roy. I'm sure you'll be fair."

"Tanner?" Roy asked.

"As long as Annie isn't judge and jury, it's okay with me," Tanner muttered, still upset by her indictment. What really smarted was that she wasn't the only one who had a right to complain. After all, she'd been the one to walk out on him lock, stock and sheet music, while he was on a grueling, six-week concert tour in Europe. She hadn't even had the courtesy to tell him she was leaving.

Well, that wasn't exactly true, he amended. She had left a message on the answering machine that said, "If this is Tanner Chapel, please be advised that I, Annie O'Neill-Chapel, have filed for divorce. You'll be served with the summons the moment you step off the plane. I never, *ever* want to see you again."

Just the memory of that message upset him, and he wanted to defend himself—to throw back a few heartfelt accusations of his own. He refrained, however, because he recognized that fighting with her would be self-defeating. She'd storm out and his plans would be shot to hell.

"And don't worry, Roy, you won't be called upon to perform this onerous duty," he added, deciding that if he couldn't fight with her, he could at least get in a dig of his own. "I wouldn't be unprofessional with Annie if you paid me. All I want to do is get the songs written for the album."

Tanner's statement hit Annie with the force of a blow. She knew she was being contrary. The last thing in the world she wanted was for Tanner to make advances toward her, but his words confirmed what she'd already begun to suspect when she'd learned the truth about him. He wasn't interested in her as a woman and probably never had been. All he cared about was that she write the words to his music.

On the tail end of that admission it suddenly occurred to her that maybe she'd misread this entire situation. Was it possible that Tanner hadn't been lying when he claimed he wasn't out for revenge? Could it be that all he was really after was her lyrical talent? Intellectually, she recognized that if that was the case, she should be relieved, because it meant he wasn't trying to sabotage her. Emotionally, however, it infuriated her to know that he was again using her creative abilities to further his career.

Well, for once she was in a position to do some using herself. Tanner was no longer an unknown, struggling singer. He was a star, and this time she'd get equal billing for his songs. Also, the more hits she wrote for him, the more exposure she would get. Then she could do exactly what she'd threatened to do—go free-lance and spend the rest of her life making sure that he never got to the top of the charts again.

Rising to her feet, she grabbed her purse and slung the strap onto her shoulder. "Since we have all the details worked out, I'm leaving. I'll be at the cabin at noon tomorrow, because the sooner we get this over with, the better. Make sure you have the kitchen fully stocked with food that you can prepare, Tanner, because I'm going to be there as a professional, not a domestic."

Glancing toward her boss, she said, "I wish I could say it's been nice seeing you again, Roy, but I'm sure you'll understand if I don't." With that she turned and walked out, barely refraining from slamming the door behind her.

When she was gone, Roy drummed his fingers against the desk top and asked, "Where are all those white doves and olive branches you promised me, Tanner?"

Tanner, who'd been frowning at the door, turned and shrugged. "I did my best, but she's being difficult."

Roy eyed him askance. "Difficult? I'd say she's mad enough to kill you, and I don't blame her. Why in hell did you keep baiting her?"

"Hey, I wasn't the one doing the baiting. You should be proud I showed such restraint."

Roy muttered a colorful curse. "If you call that restraint, we're in big trouble. I'm warning you, Tanner, if you blow this with her—"

"Save the threats," Tanner broke in irritably, "because I'm not going to blow it. As I said before, this is my career we're talking about. By the time I'm done with Annie, all our worries will be over."

"Oh, God, I know I'm going to regret asking this, but just what do you have planned for her?"

Tanner leaned forward in his chair, with a look of determination on his face and announced, "I'm going to win her back."

If Roy's earlier curse had been colorful, the one he muttered this time was positively psychedelic. "You promised you'd behave professionally toward her!"

"Yeah, well, there are some promises that are meant to be broken. Annie's mad at me, but I'm hoping that's because she hasn't let me explain what happened. Once I get her cornered at the cabin, I'll make her listen to me. Then I'm praying that she'll understand it was a foolish mistake, and that she'll find it in her heart to forgive me. If all goes as planned, we'll get married again and everything will be okay."

Roy groaned and began to massage the bridge of his nose with his thumb and forefinger. "Why did I ever get involved with crazy musicians? Why didn't I just listen to my mother and become a plumber?"

"I'm not crazy, Roy. I know exactly what I'm doing."

The older man dropped his hand and shook his head. "That's what frightens me the most, Tanner. I'm also putting you on notice that I'm not going to aid and abet you in this. I promised Annie you'd treat her professionally, and if she calls and says she's walking, I'm not going to stop her."

"Suit yourself," Tanner said, standing. "Just remember that without Annie, I can't do the album, and if I can't do it, then you're going to be out a hell of a lot of money. If we work together, then we'll all get what we want."

"You mean everyone except Annie."

Tanner stuffed his hands into his pockets and rocked back on his boot heels. "I'm convinced Annie wants this, too. I'm sure that right now she's confused, and that I just need to help her straighten everything out in her mind. I'll see you soon."

When Tanner left the office, Roy pulled open a desk drawer, grabbed a bottle of liquid antacid and removed the cap. As he took a healthy swig from the bottle, he wondered if he was setting himself up as an accessory for murder, because he suspected that that was exactly what Annie was going to do to Tanner once she realized what he was up to.

THE MOMENT HER SISTER, Lisa, walked into the apartment, Annie thrust the evening newspapers into her hands and ordered, "Read the piece of trash I've circled in red. I can't believe it. I'm going to look like a fool again!"

Lisa read the article while following Annie into the kitchen. When they got there, she tossed the paper onto the table and smoothed her short cap of windswept brown hair into place. "*You* know it isn't true that you and Tanner are reconciling, so why are you so upset about a silly gossip column?"

"I'm upset because it's starting again." Annie poured Lisa a cup of coffee and handed it to her. "You just watch," she went on in frustration as she removed a carton of milk from the refrigerator and carried it to the table. "Tanner and I are going to be on the front page of every tabloid in the country. They're going to resurrect every sordid detail of our divorce. And you know what? I'd lay odds that Tanner planted that story."

Lisa frowned as she sat down and poured milk into her coffee. "I doubt that, Annie. The public was on your side during the divorce, so resurrecting it might hurt

Tanner. Why would he take that type of chance with his career?"

"Well, if Tanner didn't do it, who did?" Annie shot back, disgruntled because she couldn't dispute Lisa's logic. It wasn't that she felt Tanner was incapable of being this underhanded, but she, of all people, understood how obsessed he was with his career. She believed it was the main reason he'd fought so hard against the divorce. His fans had considered him a happily married man, and a divorce was a blot on his precious public image.

Lisa interrupted her musing. "You know how the rumor mill is. I'm sure everyone at NCR knew that you and Tanner were in Roy's office. Speculation would have been rampant, and anyone could have called in the tip."

"I hate it when you play devil's advocate," Annie grumbled.

"Hey, it says in the big sister's job description that you must always be the voice of reason for your little sister."

"Well, in the little sister's job description it says I don't have to like it. And for the record, I don't."

"Fair enough," Lisa replied with a chuckle. Then she suddenly sobered, and her brown eyes darkened with concern. "Are you sure you can handle working with Tanner?"

"I have to handle it. The alternative is to be blackballed in Nashville, and as much as I hate admitting it, Roy's right. If I can pull this off and win a Grammy or two, no one will be able to threaten my career again. Believe me, having that security is worth tangling with Tanner. I just wish . . ."

"Just wish what?" Lisa prodded.

"That we weren't going to be working at the cabin," Annie confessed, blinking as she felt the sting of tears. She was through crying over Tanner, so why did just the thought of the cabin make her feel weepy? "After all that's happened, I know it sounds ridiculous, but Tanner and I built so many dreams at the cabin. I can't stand the thought of facing them."

Lisa reached across the table and gave her hand a squeeze. "Honey, that's exactly why I'm so worried about you going through with this. I was there when you found out the truth about him, remember? I couldn't stand seeing you hurting like that again."

Annie raised her head and smiled ruefully. "That's exactly why I need to go through with this. I'm over Tanner, but I haven't been able to really get on with my life. Maybe it's because I shut him out of it as soon as I found out what he did. Maybe if I face him, I can put the past to rest and start working on the future."

"Or maybe it will make matters worse," Lisa countered with a troubled frown.

"How could they possibly be worse?"

"Tanner could persuade you to come back to him."

Lisa's comment was so unexpected that for a moment all Annie could do was gape at her. When she realized her mouth was hanging open, she closed it. "If that's what's worrying you, forget it. In the first place, Tanner doesn't want me back—at least not as his wife. He made that perfectly clear this morning. More importantly, I wouldn't take him back if the survival of mankind depended upon it."

"That may be true, but I still have to wonder why Tanner is insisting that you work at the cabin. He has to know it will be difficult for you. Face it, Annie. If he does have some devious plan of winning you back, what better place to wear you down than where you built so many dreams together?"

"Lisa, I already told you that the reason we have to use the cabin is because he's remodeling his house," Annie reminded her impatiently.

"I think you should verify that remodeling story, Annie. It wouldn't be the first time Tanner has lied to you."

Annie rolled her eyes toward the ceiling. "Even if he is lying, it doesn't change anything. Roy will still insist that I work with him, and if Tanner wants to work at the cabin, then Roy will make us work there. Remember, Roy's allegiance rests with the star, not the insignificant songwriter."

"You are *not* insignificant!" Lisa declared. "Why, you have more talent in your little finger than Tanner has in his entire body."

Annie couldn't help grinning. "Spoken in true prejudiced sisterly support."

Lisa frowned. "I may be prejudiced, but you don't give yourself enough credit. If you were insignificant, Tanner wouldn't be pulling this stunt. Since he is, I think he's finally discovered what I've known all along. If it wasn't for you, he'd have never made it."

Annie shook her head. "He made it because he's not only a gifted musician, he has a voice most singers would kill to have. He also wanted to be a star more than anything else in the world, and it was his determination to reach that goal that made him succeed. All I did was go along for the ride."

"Don't you dare sit there and denigrate your role in his success!" Lisa exploded with such uncustomary vehemence that Annie blinked in surprise. "You worked your butt off for him, Annie. It was *you* who kept his house clean and cooked his meals and did his laundry, while he sat around strumming his guitar. It was *you* who held down two jobs to pay the bills, while he performed for peanuts in every two-bit bar between here and the middle of nowhere. It was *you* who then came home and, instead of going to bed and getting your sleep, stayed up to write the lyrics for his music. And it was *you* who believed in him and wouldn't let him give up when he became depressed and discouraged. If anyone went along for the ride, it was Tanner, and as far as I'm concerned, he should be shot for what he did—and is *doing*—to you."

When Lisa's diatribe was over, Annie glowered at her. "You make it sound like I lay down on the floor and invited Tanner to walk all over me, and that isn't true. I did what I did because I believed in his talent, and I wanted to do whatever I could to help him realize his goals. If that makes me a fool in your eyes, I'm sorry, but I am not going to apologize for doing what I thought was right."

Lisa released a heavy sigh. "Annie, I have never considered you a fool, and I apologize for making it sound as if I did. It's just that I'm tired of you making it seem as if Tanner is some musical god and you're just some peon hanging around in the wings. It's true that he can write beautiful music. It's also true that he has a singing voice that melts your insides. But you give him the words, Annie, and without those words, he can't do anything with his talents. It's time you recognize that he needs you more than you need him."

Annie shook her head. "You're wrong. There are very few people with Tanner's musical and singing talents. There are, however, tons of talented lyricists. If I don't write his lyrics, someone else will, which means I need him more than he needs me. Of course, if I handle this project right, that will definitely change."

"So you're determined to go through with it?"

"Can you honestly see any other choice?"

Lisa gave her an annoyed look. "Unfortunately, no, but I still don't like it."

"Join the club."

"Well, if you need help at the cabin, all you have to do is send me an SOS and I'll order in the cavalry."

"If I send you an SOS you'd better order a bail bondsman," Annie stated dryly, "because it will probably mean I've strangled Tanner. But don't worry about me, Lisa. I'm going to take along a secret weapon that will keep him in his place."

Lisa arched a brow. "What sort of secret weapon?"

"Pooh," Annie answered, grinning widely as Lisa broke into side-splitting laughter.

4

PLOPPING DOWN ON THE SOFA, Tanner decided that he hated cuckoo clocks. The one in the cabin had been chirping at him every half hour since he'd arrived last night. It was noon, so right now it was having a field day informing him of the hour. If he hadn't given the blasted thing to Annie as a present, he'd toss it into the fire that was flickering on the hearth. Instead, he leaned his head back against the cushions and closed his eyes. Annie should arrive any minute, but would she really come?

The question had been deviling him all morning, because he'd suddenly realized that she'd capitulated too easily. Had she been just stringing him along? Was she even now headed to parts unknown? *Damn!* Why hadn't he insisted she come up here with him last night, so he could make sure she didn't run away?

The same panic that had caused him to demolish every musical instrument in his house began to rise inside him. What if she didn't come? What if she had run away? What if . . .

He stopped himself. He was not going to panic. He was going to be in control. She'd promised she'd come, and she would, because she never went back on a promise. Once she was here, he'd make things right between them. All he had to do was stay in control. As long as he didn't lose it, everything would be okay. He wasn't going to let it be any other way.

As if scoffing at his declaration, the phone on the coffee table rang. His eyes flew open, and he slowly turned his head and stared at it with dread. Annie was the only person who'd have a reason to call him, and there was only one explanation why she would. He'd been right. *She wasn't coming.*

Frustration surged through him. He'd let her walk away from him once, and he was not going to let her do it again. They had an agreement, and she was going to fulfill it!

He snatched up the phone and without bothering with a greeting growled, "Annie, you said you'd work with me, and, by damn, you will work with me, even if I have to come back to Nashville, hunt you down and drag you up here!"

There was a long silence, and then a male voice said, "I knew it! The moment I read that damn gossip column in the newspaper, I knew Annie had seen it and backed out of the deal."

Tanner had been so sure the caller was Annie that it took him a moment to recognize the voice. "Daniel?"

"Yeah," his agent replied with a heavy sigh. "I'm sorry, Tanner. I should have read the paper last night. But don't worry. I'll call Roy right away. He can handle Annie."

A feeling of doom hovered over Tanner. He had to clear his throat to ask, "What was in the paper that would upset Annie?"

"It was just that stupid gossip column, 'Country Towne.' Nothing for you to be worried about. I'll take care of everything."

A sense of déjà vu gripped him, and he became even more worried. Those were the same words Daniel had used when the tabloids had printed the story that destroyed his marriage. "Dammit, Daniel! Don't try to pacify me. Tell me what it says!"

"Well, um, it says that you and Annie were seen together in Roy's office."

"So? Why would that upset her?"

This time it was Daniel who cleared his throat. "It also says that an inside source claims the two of you are reconciling, which, I suppose, is basically true. After all, reconciling does mean settling differences."

A knot the size of a boulder formed in Tanner's stomach. "But in gossip-column jargon, it means we're getting back together as a couple. If Annie saw that column . . . I'll kill whoever leaked the story!"

"Tanner, calm down. I said I'd take care of it."

"Just like you took care of it the last time the gossip rags started after me?" Tanner mocked. He shot to his feet and began to pace, glowering when the telephone cord brought him up short a half-dozen steps later. "As I recall, you did such a good job that I ended up in divorce court."

"That was a cheap shot," Daniel grumbled. "I did everything I could to cover up your affair, and—"

"It was *not* an affair!" Tanner broke in furiously. "It was a mistake, and you said you'd make sure that Annie never found out about it."

"Look, Tanner, this isn't the time to argue about the past. I need to get on the phone to Roy and—"

Tanner jumped when there was a knock on the door. He turned toward it so swiftly that he got tangled up in the telephone cord and nearly fell. Muttering a curse, he began to untangle himself and said, "Hold on, Daniel. Someone's at the door."

"Is it Annie?"

"How the hell would I know? I can't see through wood. With my luck, it's another damn attorney she's hired to torment me. Just hold on."

He dropped the receiver to the sofa and hurried to the door. Though he knew it was a security risk, he didn't bother looking through the peephole. With the mood he was in, any crazy fan who'd tracked him up here would be sorry.

Grabbing the handle, he swung the door open. His first response was relief. Annie was standing on the stoop, wearing an oversize yellow sweater and faded blue jeans. Her purse was slung over her left shoulder and she held a pet carrier in her right hand.

He opened his mouth to welcome her, but was interrupted by an ominous growl. It was then that the significance of the pet carrier hit him.

Warily, he lowered his gaze to the champagne-colored cat glaring out at him through the wire mesh of the cage door. When it barred its fangs at him, Tanner took a hasty step back. Annie's cat had hated him from the moment it had first laid eyes on him, and he had the scars to prove it.

Transferring his gaze to Annie's face, he snapped, "Dammit, Annie! Why in hell did you bring that blasted cat?"

She gave him a smile so sweet it was saccharine. "Why, Tanner, I knew you wouldn't forgive me if I didn't bring Pooh. I know how much you miss him. You did, after all, file for custody of him when we got divorced."

"You know perfectly well why I did that. It was the only way I could think of to make you drop your stupid divorce proceedings."

Impossibly, her smile became even sweeter. "Well, what you don't know is that I almost gave him to you."

Tanner stared at her, appalled. Just the thought was enough to make him break into a cold sweat. He glanced back down at the cat, and when he heard another growl, he didn't know if it came from the animal or from him. What he did know was that war had just been declared between man and beast.

TANNER'S RESPONSE to Pooh was exactly what Annie had hoped for, and she congratulated herself for her brilliant strategy. Bringing Pooh along was a way to get even with Tanner for forcing her to work with him. It was also a way to divert his attention from her discomfort at returning to the cabin for the first time since the divorce. It would be hard enough for her to cope without being under his scrutiny.

"Well, Tanner, are you going to let us in, or would you rather I took my cat and went home?" she asked.

His head shot up and he eyed her knowingly. "That's what this is all about, isn't it? You figured if you brought that damn cat, I'd let you back out of our deal. Well, it isn't going to work, Annie. I lived with him for ten years and survived, and I can sure as hell make it through another six weeks."

"I only agreed to one week," Annie said, correcting him. "At the end of that time I'll decide if we can continue to work together."

His expression darkened to a glower as he stepped back from the door. "Believe me, we can—and *will*—

continue to work together until this album is ready to record."

Annie entered the cabin, not bothering to respond. Since she'd already decided that it was to her professional advantage to work with him, he was right. However, she'd never admit that to him. As far as she was concerned, he could stew about it right up to the very end.

Allowing herself no more than a quick glance around the room, she set the pet carrier on the floor and crouched down to open the door. As she did so, her mind registered the fact that he hadn't changed the cabin. She couldn't decide how she felt about that. It would have been easier to face the memories if everything looked different, but it also would have hurt to know that all the hard work she'd poured into this place had meant nothing to him.

"Do you have to let him out?" Tanner questioned irritably as he slammed the front door.

"Of course, I have to let him out," Annie answered, glancing over her shoulder. "What would your fans think if they knew you were afraid of a ten-pound, fifteen-year-old pussycat named Pooh?"

"I am *not* afraid of him," Tanner denied emphatically, although Annie noted that he never took his eyes off the cat as it sauntered out of the carrier and rubbed its head against her hand.

Suppressing a malicious grin, she taunted, "Then prove it. Come over here and pet him."

"The hell I will," he muttered. "I might not be afraid of him, but as Daniel is so fond of reminding me, I need my hands to work. Oh, damn! I forgot about Daniel."

He hurried to the sofa and snatched the telephone receiver off the cushions. Turning his back on her, he spoke in a low tone.

Annie gave Pooh a scratch behind his ears and rose to her feet, deciding that she might not have another private moment to get her first real look at the room. She'd expected the experience to be painful, but it was more a sense of poignant homecoming that washed over her.

As her gaze took in the rustic log walls and the fieldstone fireplace, she wondered if she felt this way because she'd put so much of herself into the cabin. She'd sewn the lacy white curtains for the windows and crocheted the pineapple-patterned white doily that lay on the pine coffee table. Even the colorful quilted pillows on the early American overstuffed sofa and chairs had been made by her own hand. Tanner had teased her unmercifully about her domesticity, telling her that they could afford to hire a decorator, so she didn't have to waste her time. However, she hadn't considered it a waste of time. For her it had been a true labor of love.

Only now did she understand that she'd done it because the cabin had been her sanctuary. It was the only place where their crazy lives had taken on a semblance of normalcy and she could feel safe from Tanner's fans, who mobbed them wherever they went. It was the only place she'd been able to believe that the fairy-tale marriage the press claimed they shared was real.

She gave a rueful shake of her head, suddenly recognizing that even as she'd worked on the cabin she'd been fighting her instincts. Instead of acknowledging that Tanner was no longer committed to their marriage, she'd been trying to convince herself that nothing was wrong. God, she couldn't believe she'd been such an idiot!

"Annie, what's the matter?"

Tanner's voice yanked her back to the present, and she glanced toward him. He was wearing such a convincing expression of concern that for a moment she actually believed it was genuine. Thankfully, that flash of insanity was shattered by the cuckoo clock announcing the half hour. That one simple "cuckoo" reminded her that the only person Tanner cared about was himself. As the bird suggested, she'd be nuts to believe otherwise.

"You can drop the act, Tanner," she told him. "We both know that even if something was wrong, it wouldn't matter, because you don't give a damn about me or my feelings. Now, if you'll excuse me, I need to get my suitcase and Pooh's litter box and food. Then we can get to work."

She pivoted on her heel and headed for the door, and Tanner's composure snapped. Even as the voice of reason told him to ignore her barb, his extreme emotional response was propelling him after her. He was fed up with her unjust verbal attacks. All he'd done was ask her a simple question, for pity's sake!

He reached her just as she arrived at the door, and he grabbed her arm and spun her around to face him. He'd only meant to stop her from walking out until he had his say, but her feet slipped on the throw rug and she started to fall. Automatically, he linked an arm around her waist and hauled her up against him. As their bodies collided from chest to thigh, Annie let out a gasp of surprise and her eyes widened in shock.

He experienced a grim satisfaction when he felt a tremor race through her body. He'd lived with her long enough to recognize the keen edge of her lust. She might claim to hate him, but her body was telling him otherwise.

Purposely, he shifted so that her pelvis was pressed intimately against his growing arousal, and he was rewarded as another tremor shook her. When her tongue flicked nervously along her bottom lip, he began to lower his head, ignoring the nagging voice inside insisting that kissing her would be a mistake. He was just going to give her a taste of what she wanted, and then he'd sit back and wait for her to come begging for more.

ANNIE WAS SHOCKED to suddenly find herself in Tanner's arms. She knew this was wrong, but no matter how much she told herself to pull away, she couldn't. Her body was too busy enjoying the familiar crush of her breasts against the hard wall of his chest, the thrilling press of his thighs against hers, to heed her mind's warning.

Only when he began to lower his head to kiss her did she recall him telling Roy that he wasn't interested in her. So why was he making a move on her? The only reason she could think of was that he wanted to humiliate her, and he'd already caused her enough humiliation to last a lifetime.

Bracing her hands against his chest, she leaned her head back and ordered, "Let go of me, Tanner."

He gave her a smug smile. "What's the matter, Annie? Are you afraid of a little kiss?"

"What I'm afraid of is what I might catch from you."

Her jeer had the desired effect. He released her abruptly and scowled down at her. "Just what is that supposed to mean?"

"You know exactly what it means," she replied, returning his scowl as she took a step back and tugged the hem of her sweater over her hips. "You had an affair while we were married, and I shudder to think what you've been up to since our divorce."

A muscle leapt in his jaw. "I *didn't* have an affair!"

"Oh, come on, Tanner," she drawled derisively. "I may look stupid, but even I know that real babies don't come from cabbage patches."

He gave her an aggravated look. "Annie, if you'd just let me explain what happened, you'd—"

"I don't want an explanation!" she interrupted, furious with him for thinking she was so gullible he could justify what he'd done and she'd accept it. "I know all the pertinent facts, and nothing you say is going to change them.

"You also told Roy you'd behave professionally toward me," she reminded him. "So if you can't control your overactive libido, you can go prowling elsewhere. I am not interested in playing the any-port-in-a-storm game with you!"

His eyes turned a frigid blue and his expression became so darkly forbidding that Annie gulped. When he took a step toward her, she knew she should stand her ground, but she couldn't stop herself from taking a step backward. To her horror, her back collided with the door.

As he continued to advance purposefully toward her, every muscle in her body began screaming at her to run for her life. But before she could turn to find the doorknob, he came to a stop in front of her. She flinched when he propped a hand on either side of her head and angled his body forward, trapping her in place. There was so little space between them that if either of them drew in a deep breath, their chests would brush.

A tremor of sexual awareness shot through her at the thought, and she cursed silently. How could her hormones be so darned indiscriminate? Tanner might be sexy, but alley cats had better morals than he did.

She forced herself to calmly point out, "Tanner, this is not professional behavior."

"Do you think I give a damn?" he drawled softly, dangerously. "After all, I'm ruled by my uncontrollable libido, and any old port in a storm will do, even if it is my bad-tempered ex-wife."

His words were an embittered challenge, but Annie had no idea how to respond. If she agreed with his statement, she'd only make him madder. If she disagreed, she'd be implying she hadn't meant what she said, and she'd meant every word.

Suddenly, he leaned in closer. The heat from his body sent her pulse into overdrive and created a fluttering sensation low in her abdomen, so intense she trembled from the sheer wantonness of it. When he deliberately dropped his gaze to her chest, she breathed a prayer of thanks that her sweater was so baggy he wouldn't be able to see that her nipples were hard.

She sagged in relief when his gaze returned to her face. But then he began to lower his head with a calculated slowness that told her he didn't need physical proof to know how she was reacting to his nearness. She wasn't surprised. Even she could feel the sparks flying off her.

By the time his lips were no more than a hairbreadth away, she closed her eyes and tilted her head up in surrender, because, heaven help her, she wanted the unfaithful rat to kiss her! But instead of kissing her, he suddenly pushed away.

Her eyes flew open, and she stared at him in bewilderment. He'd practically forced himself on her, and she'd finally given in, so why was he pulling away?

"Sorry, Annie," he said in an arrogant drawl, "but I promised Roy I'd behave professionally toward you. So if you want to get your kicks, you're going to have to look elsewhere. I'm not into the any-port-in-a-storm game, either."

She felt a hot blush flood into her cheeks, but she didn't know if it was due to humiliation or indignation. Either way, she was so mad she wanted to kick him.

What was even more maddening, however, was that his taunt was a blatant dare for her to call Roy and report his behavior. She could just imagine Roy's response when Tanner got on the phone in turn and announced that she had all but thrown herself at him. Even if she did convince Roy that it was Tanner's fault, he'd probably tell her, "If you don't want to get burned, stay away from the fire." It would also make him less likely to side with her if she called him with another complaint—which was probably exactly what Tanner was hoping to achieve. If he cast doubt on her veracity, then he could do whatever he wanted and Roy would never let her out of the deal. Well, if he thought he could get her to cry wolf, he was wrong!

She opened her mouth to tell him off, but decided he wasn't worth the effort. Instead, she pushed herself away from the door, grabbed the doorknob and opened it.

As she started to walk out, she glanced disdainfully over her shoulder at him and, mimicking his drawl, said, "I think you misunderstood me, Tanner. I didn't say I wasn't into the game. I said I wasn't interested in playing it with *you*."

As she walked out, Tanner stared after her, stunned by her insinuation that she had an active sex life. His ego wanted to believe that she was lying—that, like him, she hadn't even been able to look at another person since the divorce. Unfortunately, he knew she was a great believer in tit for tat. He wouldn't put it past her to go to bed with another man just to get back at him.

The thought of her in another man's arms caused jealousy to hit him with such force that a red haze formed in front of his eyes. He wanted to charge after her and demand to know who she'd been with so he could track the bastard down and beat the hell out of him.

Now you know how she felt when she found out about you.

The realization was like a kick in the gut. For the first time he really understood how she must have felt when she'd seen those damning tabloid headlines. He also suspected that was why she refused to let him tell her the truth. She didn't want to hear it, because she was afraid it would hurt too badly.

He wanted to go after her and make her listen, because he was sure that the truth couldn't possibly be as painful as what her imagination had conjured up. He recognized, however, that to accept his story, she had to want to hear it.

It was a daunting revelation, because he knew she'd had a year and a half to convince herself that she hated him. He was sure she wasn't going to give up that conviction without one hell of a fight. Fortunately, he did have one thing going in his favor. The little scene he'd just played out with her proved she was still attracted to him, and though it might be unscrupulous, it was a weapon he intended to wield at every opportunity.

Filled with a new determination, he headed after her, not about to let her think she'd bested him. If she wanted a war, he'd give her one, but they were going to fight it on his terms.

5

As SHE OPENED the hatchback on her car and leaned in for her suitcase, Annie was busily dreaming up ways to get even with Tanner. She was so absorbed in her retaliatory thoughts that she let out a yelp when Tanner said, "Let me get that for you."

She bolted upright and spun around to face him, her hand pressed against her racing heart. "Dammit, Tanner! Don't ever sneak up on me like that again. You nearly gave me a heart attack!"

He gave her a properly contrite look. "I sincerely apologize, Annie. I didn't mean to startle you."

Annie eyed him suspiciously. Tanner never apologized, and she doubted he'd know the meaning of sincere if it bit him. So what was he up to now? Unfortunately, the only way to find out was to ask, and she had no illusions that he would tell her the truth.

"Fine, just don't do it again," she said, stepping back so he could get the suitcase.

When he pulled it out, she retrieved the cat's supplies and headed for the house, purposely leaving the hatchback open for him to close so she wouldn't have to walk with him.

After dropping the cat food off in the kitchen and depositing the litter box in the bathroom, she returned to the living room. Tanner was leaning against the banister at the bottom of the stairs, her suitcase still in his grip.

"I can take that now," Annie said, holding out her hand.

"I'll take it up."

"There's no need for you to do that. It isn't heavy."

He hefted the bag, as if testing the validity of her words. "It's heavy enough."

"Tanner—"

"Annie, I'm going to be a gentleman and carry the suitcase upstairs," he interrupted. "So don't argue with me."

"I'm not arguing. I'm—"

"Arguing," he broke in, as he started up the stairs. "And Roy wouldn't like that."

Annie scowled at his back. "I don't give a damn what Roy would like."

He stopped and looked down at her. "Well, I suspect that you'll give a damn if I unpack your undies, and that's exactly what I'll do if you don't get that cute fanny of yours up here."

"You wouldn't dare!"

"Annie, as you very well know, I dare to do anything I please. Now come along. We need to get you unpacked so we can get to work."

He was purposely goading her, and Annie seriously considered picking up a nearby vase and flinging it at him. The only thing that stopped her was that he disappeared up the stairs before she could grab it. Knowing that he was just despicable enough to paw through her underwear, she hurried after him.

She was halfway up the stairs when she heard a bellow and a shrill, feline howl of pain. The sounds were immediately followed by a heavy thud. With a curse, she took the remaining stairs two at a time, wondering what had happened this time. Tanner and Pooh had had a running feud from the day they'd met, and she'd never understood it. She knew Tanner liked animals, because one of the things that had attracted her to him in high school was she'd seen him feeding a couple of stray cats. Pooh's antagonism was just as baffling. Granted, he wasn't the friendliest cat in the world, but he wasn't antisocial, either. So why had it taken one look at Tanner to get his dander up?

When she reached the hallway at the top of the stairs, she saw Tanner sprawled on his back on the floor. Pooh was standing a few feet away from him and growling, the hair on his back standing on end and his tail puffed to twice its normal size.

"What did you do to Pooh?" she demanded, running to the cat and scooping him up into her arms.

"What did I do to *him?*" Tanner asked incredulously as he pushed himself into a sitting position. "That creature from hell just tried to kill me!"

She frowned impatiently. "Don't be ridiculous, Tanner. He's just a cat, and they don't try to kill people. Now, what did you do to him?"

"I can't believe this," he complained. "I could be sitting here with possible broken bones and internal injuries, and all you're worried about is that damn cat. I'm the one who fell!"

"I heard him cry out in pain, Tanner," she said, defensively. "Did you step on him or fall on him? I need to know so I can get him to the vet if he's hurt. After all, he's fifteen years old. Even a slight injury could be serious."

Tanner rolled his eyes in disgust. "No, Annie, you don't need to call the paramedics for me. I think I'll live, despite a lump the size of a goose egg on the back of my head. And if my spleen really is ruptured, I'll quietly bleed to death in my bed so I won't be a bother to you. Thank you for asking, though. Your concern is *so* touching."

She released an exasperated breath. "Tanner, I know you're okay. If you weren't, you wouldn't be complaining. Now, what did you do to Pooh? Unlike you, he can't tell me if he's hurt."

"I stepped on his tail," Tanner finally admitted, albeit grudgingly. It irked him that she always took the cat's side.

"Poor Pooh," Annie murmured, burying her face in his fur.

"Poor Pooh, hell," Tanner grumbled as he glared at the cat, who turned his head toward him and glared right back. "It's his own damn fault. All I was doing was walking down the hall, minding my own business. He was lying in wait for me behind the bedroom door, and he came running out and purposely tripped me."

This time Annie rolled her eyes. "Tanner, that's the most preposterous thing I ever heard. Cats do not purposely trip people. I'm sure he was just trying to play with you."

"When the beast finally does do me in, you'll probably have The Cat Was Just Playing engraved on my headstone," Tanner snapped as he gingerly climbed to his feet, wincing when he felt a twinge in his left knee.

Annie must have noticed his grimace, because she asked, "Are you okay?"

He shot her an aggrieved look. "Now you're showing some concern for me? Well, forget it. I'd rather suffer in stoic silence than play second fiddle to a hit-man fur ball."

He heard her let out a low chuckle and demanded, "What's so damn funny?"

She grinned. "I'm just trying to imagine you suffering in stoic silence. You might be able to master the stoic part, but the silence? No way. You like to gripe too much."

"I do not gripe!" he protested indignantly. "And I'm not going to stand here suffering in stoic *silence* while you ridicule me. So, if you'll excuse me, I'm going to limp downstairs and start to work. You can join me when you've finished consoling *poor* Pooh."

As he walked away, Annie noticed that he really was limping, and she experienced a stab of guilt. She should have shown him more concern, but he always exaggerated when it came to Pooh. To her vexation, the justification didn't appease her conscience. With a resigned sigh, she dropped the cat to the floor, and went after him, knowing that since she'd laughed at him, he'd die before he'd tell her if he was in serious pain.

"Tanner, wait."

He stopped and turned to face her, asking curtly, "What do you want?"

She stopped and raked a hand through her hair. "Look, I'm sorry for laughing at you, but I didn't realize you were really hurt. Is there something I can do?"

He shoved his hands into his pants pockets and shot a glare over her shoulder at the cat. "Well, you could turn that disciple of the devil into a pair of mittens."

"Come on, Tanner. Be serious. You're hurt, and I want you to tell me what's wrong so I can help."

He arched a brow and scoffed. "Gosh, Annie, you'd better be careful. You're actually beginning to sound as if you care."

"Dammit, Tanner! Stop playing games," she said, putting her hands on her hips in annoyance. "I know you're mad at me, but you're always so melodramatic when it comes to Pooh that I don't pay any attention to your complaints."

"I am *not* melodramatic!" he roared.

"For pity's sake, if you get a simple cat scratch, you act as if you've been attacked by a slasher, so don't tell me you're not melodramatic. I'm also not going to stand here and argue with you just because your ego got bruised. I want to know what's wrong with your leg."

When he glowered at her, she crossed her arms over her chest and tapped the toe of her shoe against the floor. "Now, Tanner."

He continued to glower, but said, "It's not my leg. It's my knee."

"Did you sprain it?" she asked, her gaze automatically dropping to the area in question.

"How the hell would I know? I'm not a doctor."

She raised her head and frowned. "You may not be a doctor, but you're old enough to know if an injury feels like a sprain or if it feels like something more serious. So answer my question."

"It feels like a sprain," he muttered.

She nodded. "In that case, we'll wrap it in a bandage, put some ice on it and keep your leg elevated. If it's not better in a day or two, I'll take you to a doctor."

Still smarting over her earlier unconcern for him, Tanner started to tell her that he didn't want her help. Thankfully, his common sense surfaced before he could voice the sentiment, because he suddenly realized this was exactly the type of close encounter he needed to start luring her into his trap. He would not only be drawing on her protective instincts, but in order for her to wrap his knee, he was going to have to drop his pants.

Not that he expected the sight of him in a pair of jockey shorts to send her into a fit of uncontrollable lust. But it would reestablish the aura of intimacy they used to share. He was sure that once he connected with her on that level, he'd be better able to move her in the direction of reconciliation.

Recognizing, however, that she would become suspicious if he accepted her help too easily, he assumed a martyred look and said, "It's nice of you to offer to help me, Annie, but I'd rather take care of myself. After all, you're here as a professional, not a nurse, and I don't want to be an imposition."

He could barely suppress his grin when she took his bait by stating impatiently, "Tanner, you know as well as I do that you can't even open an aspirin bottle by yourself. If you try to put on a bandage, you'll probably cut off your circulation, get gangrene and end up having your leg amputated. I'm going to do this for you and I don't want any arguments. Got that?"

"Well, if you're sure you want to..." he responded with what he hoped was just the right amount of uncertainty. "After all, I have to remember my promise to Roy."

She gave him an arch look. "You haven't remembered it up to this point, so I don't know why you're bothering now."

Before he could respond, she said, "Can you walk by yourself or do you need my help?"

"It is a bit painful, but it's nothing I can't stand."

"In other words, it's hurts like hell," Annie noted dryly. "Why do men always have to be so darned macho? Why can't they just admit that they're hurt and need help?"

"Because if we do, we get accused of being melodramatic," he piously supplied.

She gave him a look of aggravation. "Tanner, I swear that if you don't stop throwing my words back at me, I'm going to kick you in your other knee and then sic Pooh on you."

Just the threat was enough to make Tanner shudder, and he quickly looked for the cat. The vicious beast had disappeared, which he knew from experience was a bad sign. It meant the animal was planning his next ruthless attack.

To Annie, he said, "If you don't want a truthful answer, then you shouldn't ask the question."

She shook her head and muttered something that sounded suspiciously rude. Then she heaved a sigh and said, "Just lean on me and I'll help you to your room, and don't you dare say you can do it by yourself."

As she stepped to his side and put an arm around his waist, he draped his own arm over her shoulders and leaned heavily against her. "I can't thank you enough for doing this, Annie."

"Yeah, well, my cat tripped you, so I guess I owe you," she grumbled, leading him down the hallway. "Just don't make it a habit."

When they entered the bedroom, she led him to the bed. "Sit down and I'll get the bandage."

He nodded and reached for the waistband of his pants. When he did, she gasped, "What are you do ing?"

He glanced toward her, confused by the question. "I'm taking off my pants. How else are you going to wrap my knee?"

The look on her face was so horrified that he suddenly realized she'd volunteered her help without considering the repercussions. When her gaze dropped to his zipper, she gulped, and he had to bite the inside of his cheek to keep from grinning. Maybe he'd been wrong. Maybe just the sight of him in his underwear *would* send her into a fit of uncontrollable lust.

"Is there a problem, Annie?"

She shook her head, but her voice was barely audible as she said, "No. I'll go get the bandage. You get . . . comfortable."

As she raced toward the bathroom, he vowed to give Pooh a treat. For once the blasted cat had done him a favor, and he was going to make sure that he made the most of it.

ANNIE ENTERED the bathroom and jerked open the linen-closet door, muttering, "You've done it again! You should have thought about the consequences before you opened your big mouth. How could you be so *stupid?*"

Grabbing the plastic storage container where she'd always kept first-aid supplies, she popped off the lid. Rummaging through the box, she muttered, "If you were smart, you'd let him take care of himself. What do you care if he screws up his circulation and gets gangrene? After everything he's done to you, it would serve him right."

But even as she located the bandage and ice bag, she knew she had to go through with this. If she refused to help him, he'd suspect it was because she was bothered by the thought of seeing him half-undressed. And he'd be right.

Irritated by that admission, she headed for the bedroom, telling herself that this was nothing more than an errand of mercy. As long as she kept that in mind, she could handle seeing Tanner in his underwear.

She was so prepared for the sight that when she walked into the room and found that he'd removed his boots and socks but was still wearing his jeans, she stopped abruptly and frowned.

Before she could ask what was going on, he said, "Annie, I think I should take care of my knee myself. After all, we're no longer married, and it just doesn't seem ... well, proper that you see me without my pants."

Annie regarded him suspiciously. *Proper* was not a word in his vocabulary. "What are you up to, Tanner?"

He widened his eyes innocently. "I'm not up to anything. I'm just trying to be professional by exhibiting decorum and maintaining my modesty."

Annie made a derisive noise. "You know as well as I do that you don't have a decorous or modest bone in your body. I'm also not dense. You're playing some kind of game with me, so stop it. Now, take off your pants so I can wrap your knee."

"Well, if you insist. After all, I wouldn't want you to accuse me of being uncooperative."

Annie opened her mouth to issue a retort, but Tanner chose that moment to pop open the snap on his jeans. She automatically glanced down, and the words stuck in her throat as he began to lower his zipper with provocative slowness. She told herself to turn her back on him. Or better yet, to get the hell out of the room. But her legs wouldn't obey either command.

Her gaze was glued to his hand as she followed the zipper's descent. When he finished lowering it, he trailed his hand back to the waistband, slipped his fingers beneath the denim and then slid the other hand inside, too. As he eased his pants down over his hips, revealing a brief pair of royal blue shorts that left nothing to the imagination, her heart began to pound and her mouth went dry.

Damn! Why wasn't he wearing a shirt with long tails that covered his shorts instead of a T-shirt that did nothing to hide the fact that he was becoming aroused?

His pants hit the floor, and the sound jolted her out of her trance. She jerked her head up, and when her gaze landed on Tanner's face, she took an involuntary step back. He was staring at her with such sexual hunger that desire exploded inside her with frightening force.

This isn't supposed to be happening! she wailed inwardly, taking another step back. If she didn't, she'd probably run across the room and fling herself into his arms. Why was he doing this to her? Why was she doing it to herself?

It was as if Tanner had read her mind, because he suddenly drawled huskily, "I told you this wouldn't be proper, Annie, but you insisted."

"Well, if I'd known you couldn't behave any better than a rutting animal, I'd have sprayed you down with the garden hose first!" she returned, furious with him for again making it seem as if this was her fault.

He put his hands on his hips and glared. "Dammit, Annie! I am sick and tired of you implying that all I think about is sex."

She pointedly dropped her gaze to the front of his shorts, then looked back at his face. "Well, excuse me, Tanner. I have no idea how I could have come up with such a bizarre premise. Perhaps you have some sort of medical condition that I don't know about?"

"You're impossible!" he roared.

"I'm impossible? I offer to help you out of the goodness of my heart, and you pay me back by engaging in a damn striptease! I'm not sure what you're trying to prove, but stop playing games with me. *I am not interested!*"

Fury leaped into his eyes and he spat, "Fine! Why don't you get your suitcase and your blasted cat and go back to Nashville?"

"Fine! I will!"

She threw the bandage and the ice bag at him and marched out of the room. Tanner managed to catch the bandage, but the ice bag hit him square in the face.

Tossing the bandage aside, he snatched his jeans off the floor. While pulling them on, he muttered a curse. He couldn't believe he'd let his temper get so out of hand that he'd actually told her to leave. It was just that she was driving him crazy, particularly when she kept saying she wasn't interested in him. He'd felt the sexual tension radiating from her clear across the room. Instead of taunting her about it, he should have dragged her to bed. She was always more amenable to reason after a good tussle between the sheets.

As he limped toward the door, he cursed again, because he realized that to salvage the situation he was going to have to grovel. He hated groveling, particularly in front of Annie. She had a way of making him feel as if he was two inches tall and shrinking fast.

When he entered the hallway, he noted that her suitcase was gone. For a moment he thought he was already too late to stop her, but then he heard her downstairs, calling the cat. He turned toward the stairs, but froze when he heard a growl behind him. He glanced over his shoulder to see Pooh sitting on the windowsill at the end of the hall. The cat swished his tail when Annie called again.

Giving the cat his best threatening look, Tanner said, "If you don't want to pay a visit to the taxidermist, you'll stay up here until I've talked to her."

The cat hissed and bared his teeth, but Tanner ignored him and headed downstairs. He knew it was dangerous to turn his back on the beast, but at this point soothing Annie was more important than worrying about his backside.

He'd just reached the bottom step when Annie came out of the kitchen. "Dammit, Pooh! Come here, and come here right now!" When she saw Tanner, she said, "What are *you* doing down here?"

Her voice was filled with so much scorn that Tanner's temper flared. But he realized he needed to appease her, not inflame her.

"I came down to apologize," he said. When she didn't respond, he asked, "Well?"

"Well what?" she countered.

He frowned impatiently. "You know very well what. Are you going to accept my apology?"

"I didn't hear an apology."

He raked a hand through his hair. "You're going to make this as hard as possible, aren't you?"

"I'm not making anything hard, Tanner. I'm simply stating a fact. I did not hear an apology, and I can't accept what I didn't hear."

"All right," he grumbled. "I'm sorry, okay? Now, will you accept my apology and stay?"

She regarded him for a long moment. "I suppose that depends on what you're sorry for."

"I knew it!" he exploded. "You aren't going to be satisfied until I get down on my knees and beg. Well, one of my knees hurts like hell because of *your* cat, and I'm not going to damage it further just to quench your thirst for revenge.

"I said I was sorry," he went on, "and you either accept that or you don't. While you make up your mind, I'll hobble over to the couch where I can at least suffer comfortably."

"So much for stoic silence," she said as he limped to the sofa.

He eyed her critically as he sat down. "You have developed a vicious streak, Annie, and I must say that it isn't becoming."

She gave an unconcerned shrug. "This may come as a shock, Tanner, but I really don't care what you think about me."

"I don't believe that," he muttered as he eased his foot onto the coffee table and leaned back against the cushions. "If you didn't care, you wouldn't still be mad at me, and you'd let me explain to you what happened."

"I don't want to talk about this, Tanner," she stated tightly.

He released a frustrated sigh. "I know you don't, but have you ever considered that if you heard my story, it might not be as bad as you think?"

She laughed bitterly. "Not as bad as I think? You slept with another woman, Tanner. You had a *child* with her."

It was the emphasis she placed on the word *child* that made all the pieces suddenly fall into place for Tanner. Why hadn't he figured it out sooner?

"That's why you're so angry with me, isn't it? It isn't the affair you think I had. You could have probably forgiven me for that. What you can't forgive is that I fathered a child. Why, Annie? It's not like I wanted it to happen. I know a child is a big deal, but why does it make that much difference?"

"I told you that I don't want to talk about it!" she snapped as she walked to the window and stared outside.

Tanner gave a futile shake of his head. He now understood the problem, but he couldn't do anything to resolve it until he knew exactly why it was such a big deal for her. It was also apparent that she'd gone into her stubborn mode, which meant he wouldn't get any answers from her today. Of course, if she left he'd never get the answers, and he railed at himself for telling her to get out in the first place.

"Are you going to leave?" he asked.

She continued to stare out the window. "I should."

Tanner felt the first stirring of hope. "But you're not going to?"

She turned to face him. "No, I'm not going to, but I want you to stop playing these games with me. Our relationship is over, and we have the divorce papers to prove it."

Tanner started to say that she might have the divorce papers, but he'd burned his the day he got them. When they'd married, he'd vowed "until death do us part." As far as he was concerned they would remain married until that happened, and no piece of paper was going to change that fact.

He refrained, however, from expressing the sentiment, because he knew this was probably the one-and-only chance he'd have to make things right between them. To goad her, even with the truth, would be self-defeating.

"All right, Annie, I won't play any more games." *For now*, he added silently.

She eyed him doubtfully. "I mean it, Tanner. I'm here to work, and that's it. I don't even want to discuss the weather with you, and if you can't live with that, I'm gone."

"I guess that means I'm going to have to wrap my own knee. How long does it take for gangrene to set in?"

He was surprised by her unexpected smile. "You're incorrigible."

He grinned. "Yeah, but it's worth it, because I just discovered you still have that beautiful smile. It's been so long since I've seen it that I was beginning to think you'd lost it."

She immediately sobered. "I guess I haven't had a lot to smile about lately."

He grew serious in turn. "I guess that's my fault, and I am sorry, Annie. I never meant to hurt you."

"Well, you did." Before he could respond, she said, "I'll go get the bandage and a robe so you can exercise decorum and maintain your modesty while I take care of your knee."

"Now who's throwing words around?"

"Well, as they say, what's good for the goose . . ."

As she went up the stairs, Tanner leaned his head back and stared at the open-beam ceiling. He'd come close to blowing it with her, but at least he'd discovered the source of her anger with him. Eventually he'd get her to talk to him about it. But until that happened, he would have to move carefully with her, which would be a test of his self-control. He was accustomed to going after what he wanted with no holds barred.

He gave a disgusted shake of his head. At this stage of his life he should be sitting back and enjoying his success, not fighting to hold it all together.

6

As Tanner watched Annie rise from her chair and adjust the blinds, he absently strummed some chords, trying to figure out what was going on. They'd been in the music room for at least fifteen minutes, and she'd done nothing but fidget. First she'd opened the blinds. Then she had to get her notepad and pencil from her suitcase. When she'd returned, she'd adjusted the blinds. A few minutes later, she'd gone to check on Pooh. Now she was readjusting the blinds again.

Tanner raised his eyebrows when she turned toward him and asked, "Are you hungry? I can make you a sandwich or something."

If she was offering to feed him, something was definitely wrong. "I'm fine, thanks."

"Are you sure?"

"Yes."

"Well, how about some coffee or a soda?"

"No, thank you."

"Are you sure?"

"I'm positive. Shall we get to work?"

"Yeah, okay, but if you want something—"

"If I want something, I'll get it myself," he interrupted. "As you told me in Roy's office yesterday, you're here as a professional, not a domestic."

Color flared in her cheeks and her chin came up an indignant notch. "I know what I said in Roy's office, but that was before you injured your knee. I'm trying to be nice, Tanner. You didn't need to remind me of my words."

Tanner rubbed a hand over his face. "I didn't mean to offend you, Annie. It's just that ever since you arrived, you've been harping at me to get to work. Now that we're ready to do so, it's as if you're trying to avoid it. Is something wrong?"

"Of course not," she quickly answered, but Tanner noted that she refused to look at him. "As I said, I was just trying to be nice."

He frowned. It was obvious she was lying, but instinct told him not to call her on it. "Well, thanks for your consideration, but I don't need anything right now. Shall we get to work?"

"Sure," she mumbled, walking to her chair. She sat down, but immediately bounced back up. "I think I'll sit on the floor."

"Don't forget your pad and pencil," Tanner reminded her.

"Oh, yeah, thanks."

She grabbed the items off the end table and walked to the corner farthest from him. Sitting down, she leaned her back against the wall and drew her knees up to her chest, causing Tanner to frown again. Obviously, she was upset. What he couldn't figure out was why. He'd been a perfect gentleman since she'd agreed to stay, so what was bothering her? He wanted to ask, but since she'd already denied that there was anything wrong, he decided to maintain his peace.

He played a few more chords on the guitar before asking, "So which of the songs would you like to work on first?"

She shrugged. "It doesn't matter."

"You don't have a favorite?"

"Not really."

Her uninterested, almost bored tone pricked at his ego. According to Roy, she'd called his works masterpieces, but he'd seen her more excited about moldy leftovers in the refrigerator.

He told himself to leave it alone, but his mouth seemed to have a mind of its own. "There isn't one melody that just jumped out and grabbed you?"

Annie regarded Tanner warily. There was an edge to his voice that signaled defensiveness. She wasn't surprised. She knew she was provoking it, but she couldn't help herself. The moment they'd entered the music room, the full impact of what she'd committed herself to had hit her.

She was going to write the words to Tanner's melodies and secure her career. On the surface that seemed simple enough. But what she had failed to realize was that in order for her to write the hits she needed to reach her goal, she had to use the emotions his music evoked inside her. That meant she was going to have to reveal the heartache she'd endured during their breakup. She didn't know if she could survive the humiliation of him realizing just how badly he had hurt her, and he would definitely figure it out. He might be egotistical, but he also had an insight into people that often amazed her.

Of course, she didn't have to write the lyrics from her emotions, she admitted. She could just make something up. But if she did that, they wouldn't stand a chance of being award-winning songs. Then she'd either have to renew her contract with NCR and be at Roy's mercy the next time he decided he had an intolerable job for her, or she'd have to finish her accounting degree and give up writing lyrics altogether. Neither option was acceptable, nor was baring her soul to Tanner. So how was she supposed to resolve the dilemma?

Tanner broke into her thoughts by tautly stating, "I'm waiting for your answer, Annie."

She knew she couldn't avoid his question any longer without starting a fight, which meant she either went to work and did the best she could, or became an accountant.

Drawing in a deep breath, she said, "I don't have a favorite, because I love all your melodies equally, Tanner. As I told you yesterday, it's the best music you've ever written. And it doesn't matter which one we begin with. I have tons of notes on all of them, so you pick the one you like the best and we'll go from there."

Tanner knew he should be appeased by her answer, but he wasn't. He didn't doubt what she'd said, because he could hear the sincerity in her voice. But as she'd spoken, she'd wrapped her arms around her legs and drawn her knees in closer to her chest. She was shutting him out, and he hated it.

He was tempted to go to her, jerk her to her feet and force her to acknowledge him. The trouble was, he wasn't sure if he'd kiss her or shake her, and he knew she'd react badly to either choice. So he turned his attention to the guitar. For several moments he simply played a series of nonsensical chords, but then he closed his eyes and began to play the opening strains of one of the melodies.

"Have you got notes on this one?" he asked.

"Yes," she answered, and he heard the rustle of paper as she flipped through her pad.

He played the melody through once, and then began again, eager to hear what she'd come up with.

He didn't have to wait long, because Annie began to sing in her soft, off-key alto.

"How peacefully you slumbered
In the comfort of my arms
You'd stir and reach out for me
To protect you from any harm

At dawn you'd wake and listen
To the cooing of the doves
You'd tell me that their verses
Were the tale of our love

But then one day you left me
And the doves, they left me, too
All I have now are memories
And they simply will not do

I miss the feel of you beside me
I miss your sleep-filled sighs
I miss the way you laughed with me
I miss the way you cried

I miss everything about you
And I don't know what I did wrong
But I know that if you come back to me
The doves will come back, too

We'll spin more tales for them to coo about
At each new dawning light
Then I'll hold you and watch over you
Each long and lonely night

Oh, please, my darling, come back to me

And the doves will come back, too
Oh, yes, if you'll just come back to me
I know they'll come back, too"

As Tanner played the last note, he opened his eyes and stared at her in awe. For days he'd tried to come up with words to fit the melody and had failed miserably. Yet Annie had had the tape for less than two days and she'd practically written the entire song. Granted, there were some rough spots they'd have to work out, but they could do it in a matter of hours. If all the songs went this well, they might be done within the week!

Tanner's elation died at the thought. Though he was anxious to get the songs written, he recognized that a week wasn't nearly enough time to win Annie back. Hell, he'd be lucky to get her to discuss the weather with him in that short a time. The album was important, but getting her back was critical. Somehow he had to find a way to slow their work down so he could have some time to woo her. But how in the world was he going to do that?

"You didn't like the lyrics."

Annie's voice jerked him out of his troubled musing. "I'm sorry. What did you say?"

"I said, you didn't like the lyrics," she repeated grimly.

"Of course I like them! They're wonderful. Fantastic, even. It's just that . . ."

"Just that what?"

Tanner wanted to curse as he watched her again wrap her arms around her shins and draw her knees more tightly to her chest. He knew that if he criticized her lyrics, she'd want to change them, and he didn't want them changed, just fine-tuned. At the same time, he wanted to slow down her creative process so he'd have more time to win her back. But how in hell was he supposed to do that without making her think he hated the lyrics?

He shifted in his chair and the ice bag, which she'd filled with ice cubes and set on his knee, fell to the floor. As he started to lean forward to get it, the perfect delaying tactic came to him in a flash of pure genius.

Slumping back against the cushions, he said, "Annie, I love the lyrics. They have a few rough spots, but I know we can work them out in a matter of hours. It's just that . . ."

He purposely paused for a count of five before saying, "Oh, forget it. It isn't anything for you to worry about. Let's get back to work."

When she didn't respond right away, he thought she wasn't going to take his bait. But then she asked, "What am I not supposed to worry about?"

Once again he had to bite the inside of his cheek to keep from grinning. "It's nothing, Annie. Really. You're here to work, and that's what we're going to do."

She let out an exasperated sigh. "Tanner, if you don't answer my question in the next two seconds, I'm going to hit you with something. Now, what am I not supposed to worry about?"

"It's just my knee," he answered. "It's aching a little."

"Which in macho manspeak means it hurts like hell," she said. "Did you take some aspirin?"

"Two, but they don't seem to be helping," he cheerfully lied. "But that isn't your problem. I'm sure I'll feel better soon. We'll just keep working."

"Don't be ridiculous," she said, rising. "If you're in pain, you won't be able to concentrate properly. Maybe we should go to the doctor."

"Oh, I don't need a doctor. You know how these fresh injuries are. It takes a little time for the body to get over the shock. If you could just help me into the living room, I'll lie down on the sofa for a while. I'm sure the aspirin will kick in shortly, and then we can go back to work."

She regarded him uncertainly as she crossed to his chair and retrieved the ice bag off the floor. "I don't know, Tanner. Knee injuries are nothing to fool around with. If you're in this much pain, I think you should get your knee checked out."

"If it's not better by morning, then we can go to the doctor," he compromised.

"Let's get you into the living room," she said, taking his arm and helping him to his feet.

"I'm really sorry," he said, leaning heavily against her and exaggerating his limp as she led him toward the door. "I know you have better things to do than play nursemaid to me. If you'd like to go back to Nashville, I'll understand. I can call you when my knee is better."

"Don't be ridiculous, Tanner," she grumbled. "As you said, it will probably be better in the morning. Besides, I brought the copy of your tape with me. While you're resting, I'll listen to it and draft some lyrics for the other melodies."

Tanner nearly tripped over his own feet at that announcement. The purpose of his "injury" was to keep her from working, not encourage her to work without him!

Unfortunately, he couldn't tell her not to or she'd become suspicious. So what was he going to do to stop her? Whatever it was, he was going to have to do it fast!

"COME ON, CHAPEL, THINK! There has to be some way to keep her from working," Tanner muttered to himself as he sat on the edge of the sofa. Annie had gone upstairs to get some pillows. If he didn't have a plan before she returned, she'd go to work and there wouldn't be a thing he could do about it. There were, of course, short-term delay tactics he could use, such as having her feed him. What he really needed, however, was a way to keep her away from the tape long enough for him to woo her.

Damn! Why hadn't he remembered that she had a copy of it? Before, they'd always worked on a one-on-one basis, with him playing the music on the guitar and her composing the lyrics while he did so. Then they'd iron out the rough spots together until they came up with the perfect song. Although he knew it wasn't unusual for a lyricist to work directly from a musician's tape, he'd never considered that Annie would do it with *his* music. The way his luck was running, she'd probably go into the music room, turn on the tape, pull out her notes and have all the songs written by midnight.

But he was not going to let that happen, and he glanced around the room in search of inspiration. When his gaze landed on her suitcase, which was sitting near the front door, he realized she hadn't taken it back upstairs after he'd told her to leave. He was sure the tape was in it. She hated purses and always carried the smallest one she could find. If something wasn't es-

sential, it didn't go into her purse, and he doubted she
considered his tape essential feminine paraphernalia.

He rose and crossed to her suitcase. After ensuring
that she couldn't spot him from the stairs, he laid it on
its side and crouched in front of it, grimacing at the pull
of muscle in his sprained knee. Shifting to take off the
pressure, he reached for the latches. As he did so, Pooh
seemed to drop from the sky, landing on top of the
suitcase.

Tanner blinked when he found himself nose to nose
with his nemesis. Since he preferred to have his face in
one piece, he'd have normally backed off in a flash.
However, these were not normal circumstances. He was
a desperate man, and he wasn't about to be defeated by
a mangy cat.

Staring the beast down, he stated quietly but firmly,
"Look, it's time you get one thing straight. Annie is
mine, and nothing you do is going to change that. Now,
either you start cooperating with me, or I swear that the
day after Annie and I get married again, I'm going to
buy a pit bull to keep you in line. So, what's it going to
be?"

Pooh sat down on his haunches and tilted his head
to the side, as if considering Tanner's words. Tanner
maintained his unblinking stare, knowing better than
to show even an inkling of weakness. Evidently the cat
decided to heed his warning or, more likely, decided
that Tanner wasn't exhibiting sufficient terror to make
the game interesting. With a half-hearted growl, he
hopped off the suitcase and raced up the stairs.

"Probably running up there to tattle on me," Tanner
grumbled, popping open the latches and lifting the lid.

Since the obvious place to put the tape was in the side pouch, he searched there first, swearing when all he came up with were three pairs of socks, a pack of chewing gum and some kind of mystery novel that involved, of all things, a detective cat.

As he tucked the book back into the pouch, he concluded that he was going to have to broaden Annie's reading horizons. Maybe he'd buy her a few dozen romance novels. They supposedly always ended happily ever after. Maybe they'd give Annie some ideas about their relationship—make her see that love could conquer anything. And he was sure she still loved him. If she didn't, she wouldn't be so mad at him.

Of course, there was an added bonus to romance novels, he reminded himself. They were also supposedly good for a woman's libido—not that Annie didn't already have a healthy one. But considering her hostility toward him, a little sexy reading might tilt the scales in his favor. If he could just get her in his arms, he knew that she would finally see the light and come back to him. Nothing made a woman more open to her feelings than a good bout of lovemaking.

Just the thought of making love with Annie, of listening to her sighs and cries and feeling her silken heat surrounding him, made him aroused. But now was not the time to be thinking about *that*, he firmly reminded himself. Annie would be back any second. Hastily he searched the remainder of her suitcase. He finally found the tape tucked between a sweater and some jeans.

"Yes!" he whispered triumphantly, pulling it out and sticking it into his back pocket.

He was shutting the suitcase when he heard Annie coming down the stairs. With another curse, he tried to close the latches. One caught, but he didn't have time to worry about the other. He set the case upright and hurried back to the sofa, plopping down on it a split second before she appeared.

"What's wrong?" he asked when she frowned at him.

"You look flushed. Are you running a fever?"

"No. It's the fire. It makes it awfully warm in here."

"I thought it was rather chilly. I'd forgotten how cold it can be in the mountains in April," she said, walking to the sofa and dropping a half-dozen pillows on it. She reached out and placed a hand against his forehead. "You feel a little warm. Maybe I should take your temperature."

"I sprained my knee. I don't have the flu."

"Well, it wouldn't hurt to take your temperature anyway. Lay down and tuck a couple of these pillows under your knee. I'll be right back."

Tanner started to object, but the tape poked him in the buttock, reminding him that he needed to get her out of the room so he could hide it. "If you think that's best."

The moment she was gone, he bounded off the sofa and hurried to the mantel, ignoring the twinge in his knee. There was a silk floral arrangement on it, and he pulled the flowers out of the vase, dropped the tape inside and reinserted the flowers. He barely made it back to the sofa before he heard her coming again.

Grabbing half the pillows, he tossed them against the sofa arm. Then he tucked the remainder beneath his knee. He'd just managed to lie down when she walked into the room.

Returning to his side, she gave the thermometer a few shakes, checked the temperature gage, shook it a cou-

ple more times and then held it out for him. He obediently opened his mouth.

As she placed it beneath his tongue, she asked, "What
time did you take the aspirin?"

Tanner had never figured out why she always asked
a question after she stuck a thermometer in his mouth.
It was as ludicrous as a dentist trying to carry on a conversation with his hand crammed halfway down your
throat. Knowing she'd scold him if he removed the
thermometer, he held up two fingers.

She glanced at her watch. "That's just a little over an
hour ago, so we don't dare give you any more right
now. Is the pain easing at all?"

He shook his head, chagrined to realize it wasn't a lie.
His foray into her suitcase and his hasty trip to the
mantel had made his knee begin to throb. Great. He'd
probably end up with a serious injury while trying to
fake one.

"Are you sure you don't want to go to the doctor?"

He shook his head.

"Okay, but if you aren't better in the morning, I'm
phoning for an appointment, and I'm not going to argue about it."

He nodded.

She was evidently satisfied, because she adjusted the
pillows beneath his knee and then placed the ice bag on
it. When she was done, she glanced at her watch again.
"You have another minute. While we're waiting, I'll get
the tape out of my suitcase."

Tanner recalled the open latch and nearly swal-
lowed the thermometer. *Dammit it all to hell!* Why
hadn't he remembered to close it while she was out of
the room?

She was heading for the suitcase when the phone rang. It was so unexpected that, startled, he bolted upright. Annie immediately swung around, saying, "I'll get it. You lay back down and keep the thermometer in your mouth."

Tanner obediently complied with a thankful sigh. It was probably Daniel or Roy calling, and he could ask her to leave the room. That would give him time to secure the latch, and she'd never be the wiser.

Annie answered the phone and said, "Hank! Of course you're not being a pest. I told you you could call me here anytime."

Tanner scowled. Who the hell was Hank? And what right did she have giving out *his* phone number and telling the bastard he could call her here anytime he wanted?

She was silent for a moment and then let out a throaty chuckle. Thankfully, she reached over and removed the thermometer from Tanner's mouth as she did because his teeth automatically clenched at the sound.

She laughed at something "Hank" said as she looked at the thermometer. Then she laid it on the end table, not even bothering to look toward Tanner to indicate if his temperature was normal. He barely refrained from snatching the receiver out of her hand and slamming it down. Once she was off the phone, however, she was going to get a good piece of his mind. She was up here to work with him, not carry on with some . . . some *Hank!*

"Sure," she said. "Just hang on a minute. I need to go into the other room where it will be more private."

Holding the receiver toward Tanner, she said, "I'll take this call in the other room. Would you please hang up when I get on the extension?"

Everything male in Tanner told him to refuse her request, but he knew he'd look foolish. Sitting up, he took the instrument, muttering, "Sure. By the way, what was my temperature?"

"Ninety-nine," she answered, heading for the music room without a backward glance. "I'll let you know when I'm on the line so you can hang up."

Tanner stared after her, flabbergasted. He had a temperature of *ninety-nine?* That was four-tenths higher than normal, which meant he was running a fever, and all she was worried about was getting back on the phone with her—her... He couldn't bring himself to assign a name to her relationship with Hank, because the ones coming to mind were too unsettling.

She finally came on the line and said, "You can hang up now, Tanner."

Although he would have liked to stay on long enough to hear his rival's voice, he dropped the receiver into place and glared at the phone. What could Hank possibly have to say important enough for her to leave him lying here burning up with a fever? If he'd had any misgivings about faking his knee injury or stealing the tape, they were gone. Annie was his, by damn, and she wasn't leaving here until she accepted that fact.

With grim resolve, he went and fastened her suitcase. Then he returned to the sofa and began to plot, vowing that by the time he was through with her, she wasn't going to remember her own name, let alone a silly one like *Hank*.

7

ANNIE GAVE AN AMUSED shake of her head as she hung up the phone, deciding that the country-and-western-music business was never going to be the same after Henrietta "Hank" Mendez made her debut. She was a talented singer and musician, but it was her bawdy sense of humor that would make her a household name. She wasn't crude, but every sentence she spoke contained a sexual innuendo. She could make taking out the garbage sound like exquisite foreplay.

Normally Hank was the kind of woman Annie hated on sight—exotically beautiful, outgoing and self-assured. For Hank, shy probably meant turning your back on a stranger while you stripped down to nothing. But after spending five minutes with her, Annie had known she'd found a friend for life. Hank was flamboyant and outrageous, but she was also a warm, down-to-earth woman.

Writing lyrics for Hank's songs had been a challenge for Annie. She'd recognized that though the words had to fit the singer's sexy outward appearance, they also needed to reflect her inner spirit. Annie felt she'd done exactly that, and soon they'd find out. Hank's album would hit the stores this week, which was why she'd called. She was having predebut jitters and had needed a friend to reassure her.

Annie prayed that Hank's album would be a success, not only for her friend's sake, but for her own. Since the world didn't know she'd written Tanner's lyrics, this would be the first time she'd be getting name recognition. If Hank's album did well, then anything good that happened with Tanner's new album would be icing on the cake. But if she wanted that icing, she was going to have to get to work, she reminded herself, rising from the chair and heading for the living room.

When she entered it, Tanner glanced toward her and drawled, "Did you enjoy your visit?"

There was an underlying rancor in his tone that made Annie stop in the middle of the room and regard him warily. It was obvious he was upset, but why? "As a matter of fact I did."

"How long have you known Hank?"

"About ten months."

His jaw dropped in disbelief. "Our divorce wasn't even final ten months ago!"

Annie was momentarily confused by his statement, but then it dawned on her that he thought Hank was a man. She started to correct his misconception, but changed her mind. Although Tanner had promised to behave, she didn't trust him. He had an ego the size of Mount Everest, and she wouldn't put it past him to try to seduce her just to prove to her that he could. If he thought there was another man in her life, he might take her rebuffs more seriously and leave her alone.

"Our divorce may not have been final, but we'd been separated for several months by the time I met Hank. I'm sure you'd gotten on with your life by then, and I was merely getting on with mine," she said, deciding that it wasn't a lie. Hank had been her first assignment at NCR. At the time, she hadn't been sure she could do it. It had been a relief to learn that she could, so she had, in effect, been getting on with her life.

Tanner's lips settled into a grim line. "Well, I hope you remember that you're up here to work, not to spend all day on the phone with Hank."

His chastisement irked her. "Believe me, Tanner, I'm well aware of why I'm here, which is why I'm going to work right now."

"Good," he said, folding his hands across his stomach and closing his eyes. "After all, I have a deadline to meet."

Although she knew she was being contrary, his comment stung. She wanted nothing more than to get the job done so she could get as far away from him as possible. However, he had again brought home the fact that he was using her talent to further his career and, as far as he was concerned, nothing else mattered.

Her temper stirred, but she reined it in. Getting mad wouldn't solve anything. It would just result in another confrontation and delay her further. Grumbling to herself, she headed for her suitcase. She'd show him. She'd get the tape and write his damn lyrics so fast his head would spin. A few minutes later, however, she sat back on her heels and stared at her open suitcase in confusion. She was sure she'd packed the tape, but it wasn't there.

"So where is it?" she mumbled.

"Did you say something?" Tanner asked.

She glanced over her shoulder at him. "I was talking to myself."

"Oh. Anything wrong?"

He was wearing such an innocent expression that she narrowed her eyes suspiciously. "I can't find the tape. I don't suppose you've seen it."

"Why would I want your tape?"

He had her there, and she turned back to the suitcase and searched it again. When she still couldn't find it, she gave a frustrated shake of her head. She was positive she'd packed it.

"Maybe it's in your purse," Tanner suggested.

She was sure it wasn't, but rose and grabbed her purse off the nearby end table anyway. A quick look assured her that the tape wasn't there.

Looking at Tanner hopefully, she said, "I don't suppose you have a copy with you."

He shook his head. "Sorry, but you know I only make a tape because Daniel insists. Once I've written the music, it never leaves my head, so I didn't even think to bring a copy with me."

Annie heaved an irritated sigh. "I can't believe this. I was so sure I put it in my suitcase."

"Well, obviously you didn't. But don't worry about it," he said magnanimously. "I'm sure I'll be better tomorrow. Of course, if you really want to work today, you could just bring me my guitar. I can probably shut out the pain, although I might have a little trouble concentrating with this fever."

Her eyes narrowed. "What fever?"

He gave her an annoyed look. "The one you said I had, remember? It was ninety-nine degrees."

"Ninety-nine degrees is not a fever, Tanner."

"Of course it's a fever. It's higher than normal."

"For pity's sake, your temperature could go up that high from just a little exertion," she said in exasperation.

"I was not exerting myself," he objected quickly. "I was sitting right here on the sofa waiting for you to bring down some pillows. And as you'll recall, you're the one who noticed that I looked flushed."

"And you're the one who pointed out that it was awfully warm in here because of the fire," she countered.

"And you said it was chilly," he returned. "I'm probably coming down with the flu or something."

"It isn't flu season, and you aren't showing symptoms of a cold."

"Fine," he groused. "There's nothing wrong with me, so go get my guitar. I don't want you to be put out."

"I'm not saying nothing is wrong with you, Tanner," she said. "I'm simply pointing out that a ninety-nine-degree temperature is not something to be concerned about. I also know your knee hurts, and I am not going to ask you to work while you're in pain. So let's stop fighting about this, okay?"

"I'm not fighting," he retorted. "I'm simply trying to be professional."

Annie raised a hand to her temple. As she began to massage it, she wished she'd never heard the word *professional*, let alone used it. He was starting to beat it to death.

"You can be professional tomorrow," she finally said. "I want you to rest for now. Is there anything I can get you?"

"I don't want to impose on you."

"You're not imposing. I'm offering."

"Well, in that case, I could use some chicken soup. That's good for a fever, right?"

Annie rolled her eyes. "Chicken soup is good for everything. The question is, do you have any here?"

"I think there's a can somewhere."

"Great. Is there anything else I can do for you?"

"My ice bag feels like it needs more ice."

"I can handle that," she said, taking it off his knee. "Anything else?"

"I think that will do it."

"Okay. I'll be back shortly."

As she walked out of the living room, Tanner grinned triumphantly. Step one in his plan had worked. He'd not only stopped her from working, he'd gotten her back into her nursing mode and taken her mind off Hank. Now he had to figure out step two, but he had until tomorrow morning to do that. Tonight he'd just lie around looking pitiful.

He reached over and turned on the radio, and barely refrained from letting out an exuberant whoop when the local weather report came on. They were predicting a late-spring ice storm to arrive in the middle of the night and last for two or three days. Already they were putting out a travel advisory, which meant he could delay a trip to the doctor. Annie was terrified of driving on ice, and with his "knee injury," there was no way he could drive. It looked as if the Fates were on his side, and he lay back down, smiling in contentment as he began to work out the details of the seduction of his ex-wife.

"I CAN'T BELIEVE I'm doing this," Annie grumbled to herself as she rinsed the dinner dishes and loaded them into the dishwasher. "All I've done today is cook and fetch and play nursemaid to an obnoxious thirty-one-year-old baby. I am such a fool."

Pooh, who was eating, looked up from his food bowl and meowed.

Wrinkling her nose at him, she said, "Don't you dare agree with me. This is all your fault. You're the one who tripped him, and—"

Her harangue was interrupted by Tanner yelling, "Annie?"

"If he wants another cup of tea or asks me to take his temperature again, I'm going to strangle him," she muttered, shoving the last dish into the dishwasher and slamming the door. What really irked her was that she wasn't as annoyed with him as she was with herself, because part of her was enjoying taking care of him. Had she lost her mind?

It was a good possibility, she acknowledged as she headed for the living room. Just then the lights flickered overhead, and she frowned. It had been raining for the last several hours, and the pinging sounds against the cabin indicated that the rain was turning into ice. She hoped the flickering lights didn't mean the power was going to go out. It was hard enough dealing with Tanner's constant demands with the power on. If they had to rough it, she'd end up killing him for sure.

She was just walking into the living room when he again yelled her name. "You can stop bellowing, Tanner," she said with asperity. "It takes me a minute to respond to your beck and call, but I do come when summoned. So what do you want *now?*"

He gave her a wounded look. "I'm sorry. I'm being a pest. Just forget I called you."

Annie closed her eyes and counted to ten. He'd also been playing the I'm sorry, forget-I-called-you game with her all afternoon and evening, and it was as maddening as his demands were. How could she have forgotten what a pain in the neck he was when he was bedridden?

After she was sure she had her temper under control, she opened her eyes and said, "Since I'm already here, why don't you tell me what you want?"

He looked as if he'd object, but she sent him a warning glance. Evidently he got the message, because he said, "I feel like I'm getting chilled, and I wondered if you would get me a blanket."

"I'll do better than that," she said, heading for the staircase for what seemed like the hundredth time in the past few hours. "I'll get you two. Can you think of anything else you might need while I'm upstairs?"

"A blanket should do it."

"Fine."

She'd put her foot on the first step when he said, "Annie?"

"What?" she asked irritably, not even bothering to look at him.

"Thank you for taking such good care of me. I really do appreciate it."

"Yeah, well, you're welcome," she mumbled, feeling a stab of guilt for taking her frustrations out on him. It wasn't his fault Pooh had tripped him, and it sure wasn't his fault that she was mad at herself for wanting to take care of him.

When she reached the top of the stairs and walked to the hall closet, she said, "There's no doubt about it. You have lost your mind. He's a rat who humiliated you in

front of the entire world. Instead of wanting to take care
of him, you should be looking for the nearest cliff and
throwing him over it."

Unfortunately, the lecture didn't alleviate her feelings. She suspected it was because this was the first time
he had really needed her since he'd become a star. Up
to that point, she'd been the one who had held everything together, while he struggled to fulfill his dream.
When his struggle ended, so had her role as caretaker.
She'd spent so many years meeting his needs and fighting for his dreams that when the demands were gone,
she'd discovered she had no identity of her own.

But that had been before, and this was now, she reminded herself. She was no longer an extension of him,
but an independent woman who did have her own
identity. She was *not* going to sabotage her newfound
independence by indulging in an absurd yearning to be
needed by him, she told herself firmly.

Grabbing a couple of thermal blankets out of the
closet, she went back downstairs, deciding that the best
way to deal with this situation was to treat Tanner the
same way she'd treat a stranger under the same circumstances. She'd be cheerful and accommodating, but
she wouldn't let it get personal.

"Here are your blankets," she announced when she
entered the living room.

"Thanks," Tanner said. "I won't bother you again
tonight."

"It's no bother," she responded, dropping one blanket on a chair and unfolding the other one.

She started to drape it over him, but one end fell to
the floor and her foot somehow got tangled in it. She
stepped back to extricate herself, and as she did, the

lights went out. Startled, she bumped into the coffee table, which threw her off balance. As she started to fall backwards, she felt Tanner's hand grab her arm and pull her forward. The next thing she knew, she was sprawled on top of him.

"Are you okay?" he asked, his voice gruff.

The lights were still out, but the embers in the fireplace gave off enough illumination for her to see his face. She could only nod in answer, because the heated glow in his eyes told her that he was as aware of the press of her body as she was of his.

"My knee," he said huskily, shifting so that they fit more intimately together.

A sudden tremor shook Annie, and feelings she'd thought long dead stirred inside her. How many times had they lain just like this in this very room? Too many, and the memories teasing at her mind were so seductive they made her ache to the core with longing.

It was as if he read her thoughts, because he whispered, "Ah, Annie, I've missed you so much."

He brushed a hand against her cheek, then slid his fingers into her hair to cradle the back of her head in his hand. When he began to draw her mouth to his, Annie knew she had to get away from him. But even as she placed her hands against his chest to lever herself up, his lips met hers in a kiss that stole the breath from her lungs and the strength from her limbs.

Any remaining resistance melted, and she groaned in anticipation as she parted her lips to his tongue. He accepted her response with a ravenous urgency. Overwhelming desire spiraled through her, and she automatically slid her legs around his hips to straddle him.

This time he groaned as he swept his hand down her back and cupped her bottom, pulling her tightly into his erection, and Annie knew she was lost. While he continued to kiss her, she curled her fingers into the front of his T-shirt and instinctively rocked her hips against his hardness.

Her mind began screaming, *This is wrong! You can't do this!* She was, however, so lost in the incredible friction happening between their bodies that she refused to heed the warning. Jerking her lips from his, she buried her face between his neck and shoulder, gasping as she felt herself whirling toward a climax.

"That's it, sweetheart," Tanner encouraged hoarsely, tightening his arms around her and beginning to grind his hips against hers. "Melt for me, honey. I need you to melt for me. Don't fight it. Just let go and melt for me."

If he hadn't started urging her on, Annie probably would have done exactly what he wanted, but his encouragement hit her like a slap in the face. *The man had cheated on her! He'd had a child with another woman! How could she lie here and let him do this to her? Had she no pride whatsoever?* Desire died as quickly as it had been born, and angry humiliation flooded through her.

"Let go of me, Tanner," she ordered furiously, raising her head and bracing her hands against his shoulders.

Tanner had been so caught up in Annie's runaway passion that he didn't realize anything was wrong until she spoke. Even then it took a moment for her words to connect with his brain. By the time they did, she was already starting to pull out of his arms, and the look of utter rage on her face told him that if he let her go, she'd be gone so fast he wouldn't even see a blur. His instincts told him that if she left the cabin, he'd lose her forever. And he couldn't afford to lose her, because he couldn't survive without her.

As she tried to get up, he tightened his hold on her and rolled so that she was trapped between him and the back of the sofa. His knee rebelled at the action, but his whole future was at stake, so he was barely aware of the pain.

She renewed her struggle with such vigor that he had to lean heavily against her to keep her from knocking them both onto the floor. "What the hell is wrong with you?" he rasped. When she tried to slap him, he caught her wrist in his hand and anchored it above her head.

"Let me go!" she screamed.

"I'll let you go when you tell me what's wrong!"

"You're what's wrong! *I hate you!*"

She made the claim with such vehemence that Tanner might have believed her if the firelight hadn't picked up the sheen of tears in her eyes. He had enough personal experience with hate to know that by the time you reached that stage, there were no tears left to cry.

Recognizing that the smartest thing to do was go with the flow until she calmed down enough to talk rationally, he said, "All right, you hate me. Would you mind telling me why?"

"You know why!"

He shook his head. "No, Annie, I don't."

"Well, if you don't, I'm sure as hell not going to tell you, so let me up," she demanded, trying to pull her wrist out of his grasp.

"I'm not going to let you up until you tell me what's going on here," he countered, tightening his grip. When she glared at him in silent belligerence, he gave a resigned shake of his head and said, "I'll make you a deal. I'll let you up if you promise you'll sit down and talk to me."

"I don't have anything to say to you!"

"You're furious with me, which means you have plenty to say, but you'd rather run away than confront me," he shot back. "Well, I'm not going to let you get away with it this time. You're going to confront me if I have to hog-tie you to make you do so. So what's it going to be, Annie? Do we do this the hard way or the easy way?"

The look she gave him now was downright murderous. "If you want a confrontation, I'll give you one you'll never forget. So let me up, and let me up now!"

"Only if you promise you won't try to run away. I mean it, Annie. I want your word that you're going to sit down and talk this out with me."

A series of emotions flickered across her face, but the firelight was too dim for him to interpret any of them. Finally, she grudgingly said, "I won't run away."

On the surface it sounded as if she was giving him what he wanted, but Tanner had lived with her too long not to be able to read between the lines. She was agreeing to stay, but she wasn't agreeing to talk. He considered forcing the issue, but decided not to press his luck. As long as she was here, he could figure out a way to make her open up to him.

Releasing her wrist, he rolled away from her and sat up. She scrambled off the sofa and was halfway across the room before he could blink. At first he thought she'd lied and was going to leave. Then he realized that she wasn't heading for the door but the window. When she reached it, she pulled open the curtains and stared out into the night.

Although Tanner had been subliminally aware of the storm outside, only now did the howling of the wind and the tattoo of frozen rain against the windowpane consciously register. It was an oddly forlorn sound that somehow fit the stiffness of Annie's posture.

As he stared at her back, which looked so slender and frail in the indistinct glow from the fire, he started to rise to go comfort her. But then he sat back down. He knew she wouldn't let him console her. She was no longer his wife, so she would no longer accord him that right.

For the first time the full impact of their divorce hit him, and he was sure that if he hadn't been sitting, his knees would have buckled and he'd have found himself lying on the floor. He'd known all along how miserable he was without her, but only now did he understand how much he'd lost. He not only needed her, but he wanted the right to comfort her, to be there for her, as she'd always been there for him.

With a weary sigh, he leaned his head against the cushions and let his mind replay what had happened between them. What had set her off? She'd been putting the blanket over him, and then the lights had suddenly gone out. He wasn't sure what had happened then, but she'd begun to fall. Automatically, he'd made a grab for her and she'd ended up in his arms. He'd expected her to leap to her feet in indignation, and when she hadn't, he'd done what any man would have done when he found the woman he loved in his arms. He'd kissed her, and from there, nature had taken its course.

Only at some point nature had obviously taken a wrong turn, and Annie had ended up furious with him.

But it had been more than anger, he acknowledged, remembering the tears that had been in her eyes. One of the things he'd always admired about her was that she was a fighter. The only times he'd ever seen her succumb to tears, she had been hurting pretty badly. For the life of him, he couldn't figure out why she was hurting so much now. He also knew there was only one way to find out.

"What did I do wrong, Annie?" he asked softly, plaintively. "All I was trying to do was love you."

8

ALL I WAS TRYING TO DO was love you. The words chased themselves around inside Annie's head until she thought she'd go mad.

It was the word *try* that was tearing her to shreds, because she suddenly realized that that was the difference between them. She'd never had to *try* to love him. For her, loving him had been as natural as breathing. From the time she was sixteen years old he'd been the pivot of her universe, the essence of her soul. She would have—and had, for that matter—sacrificed everything for him. Then he'd done the unthinkable, the unforgivable. He'd shattered the one-and-only dream she'd permitted herself, the one-and-only dream that would have allowed her to hold onto him.

As the pain of that admission welled up inside her, she fought against the tears burning her eyes, but they began to roll down her cheeks anyway. On their heels came the first sob. It was out before she could stop it, and it was followed by another and another until she felt as if she were emitting one long wail of grief.

"Dear God, Annie! What's wrong?" Tanner asked, suddenly appearing at her side.

When he placed his hand on her shoulder, she jerked away from him so quickly that she nearly fell again. Through the blur of her tears, she saw him reach out to catch her. She managed to right herself before he could, and she backed away from him frantically, unable to bear his touch because she wanted—*needed*—it so badly.

At that moment, Annie realized the most painful and shameful fact of all—that she'd been fooling herself all these months. As much as she wanted to, she didn't hate him. She was still in love with him.

If she'd hurt before, she was now in agony at that admission, and she wrapped her arms around her middle and sank to the floor. She couldn't stop the tears. She couldn't stop the sobs. And, heaven help her, as much as she wanted to, she couldn't stop herself from loving him. *Damn him! Damn him! Damn him!*

As Annie sat down on the floor and began to cry uncontrollably, Tanner decided he'd never felt so helpless or been so frightened. He'd never seen her fall apart like this, not even when her father died.

He wanted to snatch her off the floor and into his arms, but then he recalled how she'd recoiled from him moments earlier. Seeing her like this was killing him, but she obviously didn't want his solace. That cut him so deeply that he felt a lump lodge itself in his own throat.

Turning away from her, he assumed her former position at the window and stared out into the darkness, trying to get his own roiling emotions under control. What had he said or done that had made her so distraught? The answer remained elusive, and with a weary sigh, he rested his forehead against the cold pane of glass, wishing he could go back in time and take back the kiss that had sent her off the deep end. Or better yet, that he could go back and change that one fateful night that had destroyed their lives.

But he couldn't. All he could do was go forward, and it looked as if he was going to screw up his future as badly as he had his past.

"You sh-should be ly-lying d-down," Annie stammered behind him. "You—you'll h-hurt your kn-knee."

With a disbelieving shake of his head, Tanner swung around to face her. Her crying had subsided somewhat, but she was still sobbing enough that she could barely breathe. But instead of worrying about catching her breath, she was concerned about his damn knee.

The only reason guilt didn't reduce him to a puddle on the floor was that their wrestling match on the sofa had played hell with his knee. Indeed, it hurt so badly that he wouldn't be surprised to learn that he *did* have a serious injury. Right now, even he had to admit that that would be poetic justice.

"I'll lie down if you'll come sit on one of the chairs," he told her.

When she gave a vehement shake of her head, he said, "The power's out, Annie. That means the furnace is off, and I don't know if you've noticed, but even with the fire, it's getting damn cold in here. If you continue to sit on the floor, you're liable to make yourself sick. Please, let me help you to a chair. I promise that once you're there, I won't touch you again or even look at you, okay?"

She glanced up at him, and his heart broke at the sight of her red, swollen eyes and puffy face. He was aching with the need to hug her close and promise her that he'd cut off both his arms before he ever hurt her again.

Instead, he held out his hand and waited to see if she'd accept his help. For a long moment it looked as if she wouldn't, but then she finally took it. Tanner had never felt more humbled in his life, because he knew instinctively what it had cost her to give him that tiny amount of trust.

He led her to the chair where she'd tossed the other blanket. Grabbing it, he shook it open, wrapped it around her and then urged her to sit. As she did so, he was relieved to note that she seemed to be regaining control. She was now down to sniffs and hiccups.

When she was settled, he asked, "Would you like some water?"

"N-no th-thanks," she said, wiping a hand across first one tear-stained cheek and then the other.

"Are you sure? I don't mind getting it for you."

"I—I'm s-sure."

"Okay, but if you change your mind, just let me know."

She nodded and leaned back in the chair, closing her eyes.

Tanner limped to the fireplace and tossed more wood on the fire. He hadn't been kidding when he'd said it was becoming cold, and he cursed himself for not getting around to installing a generator to handle such emergencies.

Returning to the sofa, he snatched his blanket off the floor and sat down. After easing his feet to the coffee table, he spread the blanket over his lap, leaned back and stared at the fire. He'd have preferred to stare at Annie, but he'd said he wouldn't look at her. He was determined to keep his word.

But even though he didn't look at her, he was aware of every nuance of her mood. He followed each stage of her calming process until she was breathing softly and steadily. Only then did he let himself begin to relax.

He had no idea how much time passed, but it seemed like forever before she hesitantly said, "Tanner?"

"Yes?" he replied, forcing himself to keep his gaze trained on the fire.

"Why did you do it?"

Her question was so generic that it could have applied to anything, but Tanner intuitively knew what she was asking. After all this time, she wanted to hear the real story about his alleged affair.

At any other time he'd have been jubilant that she'd finally decided to hear the truth. Tonight, however, he'd watched her fall apart, and he wasn't sure she was strong enough to handle it right now. Granted, it wasn't anything like the tabloids reported, and he still felt that it would hurt her less than what her own imagination had probably conjured up. But he also recalled it was the child that was at issue for her. Since he didn't know why it bothered her so deeply, he was leery about telling her the story. For all he knew, it might send her into another crying jag, and he couldn't stand the thought of that.

Slowly he rolled his head toward her. She was curled up in the chair, her feet tucked under her and the blanket wrapped around her. Her hair was in a wild tangle, and her eyes were still swollen, her face puffy. She'd never looked more beautiful or more vulnerable to him, and every protective instinct he possessed surged to the surface. He'd give his life to make her happy, but he couldn't make her happy without hurting her first.

"I don't think tonight is the right time to talk about this, Annie."

"I think tonight is the perfect time, Tanner. I want—no, I need—to understand. Please."

Tanner was still hesitant, but there was a look of quiet determination on her face that told him she wasn't going to let it go. She wanted to know, and she'd badger him until he told her.

"All right," he said, turning his head back so that he could again stare at the fire while trying to figure out where he should begin.

DEAR LORD, WHAT IS happening to me? Annie wondered in bewilderment. *I was sure I'd shed all the tears I was going to shed over him, and yet I just made a complete fool of myself by falling apart in front of him. Now I'm sitting here practically begging him to give me the gruesome details of his affair. Why am I doing this to myself?*

She wasn't sure of the answer. Perhaps she was looking for a reason to hate him so she wouldn't have to love him. Or perhaps she needed to understand so she wouldn't want to hate him.

Or maybe it's because you want him back, her mind suggested.

Annie gave an inward shake of her head. She may have come to accept that she still loved Tanner. She might even be able to accept his story and forgive him. But she would never consider going back to him. When he'd been struggling, they'd been a team. Now he was a star, and the inescapable truth was that he didn't need her any longer. At least he didn't need her in the way she wanted to be needed, she amended.

For him, his career came first and foremost. True, he needed her to write his lyrics, but he'd only record an album every year or two. That left massive blocks of time when she would be no more than excess baggage. He didn't even need her to cheer him on, because he now had millions of adoring fans.

There were also other aspects of his life she hadn't been able to come to grips with, she admitted. He adored the mobs that swarmed over him everywhere he went, and she was claustrophobic in crowds. He loved posing for cameras, and she was camera shy. And though he'd probably deny it, she suspected he more than enjoyed the sexy and often-talented women who came on to him. Even if he hadn't cheated on her, Annie would have probably ended up accusing him of doing so, because that was a threat to her femininity she couldn't seem to handle.

No, she didn't want him back, because she knew he could never be devoted to her in every way. But because she did still love him, she didn't want to lose him entirely, either. Maybe if she could forgive him, they could remain friends. Then she could continue to write his lyrics and be a small part of his life. It was a bitter pill to swallow, but she knew that hearing his story was the only medicine that was going to let her get on with her life. So she rested her head against the chair back and waited for him to begin.

When he shifted so he could stretch his legs out on the sofa, she automatically ordered, "Put the pillows under your knee and the ice bag on top of it."

He smiled wryly as he did as she instructed. Then he settled back against the sofa arm and stared at her as he announced, "It happened the night my mother died."

His words came as such a shock that Annie could only gape at him. She'd been prepared for many possibilities, but that one had never entered her mind. It also sent a chill down her spine, because she knew how ambivalent his feelings were toward his mother. Personally, she'd never understood why he had anything to do with the woman. She'd been a mean, vindictive drunk who'd emotionally abused him from birth.

Evidently, he didn't expect a response from her, because he raked his hand through his hair and continued, "I can't tell you how many times I've relived that night in my mind. I have a million excuses, Annie, but I'm not going to insult you by giving you excuses. You deserve the truth, which is why I'm going to tell you the entire sordid story from beginning to end. I have to warn you, however, that there are things I'm going to say that are not only going to hurt you, but will probably make you mad as hell at me. Are you prepared to deal with that?"

"Yes," she answered, knowing that she was telling the truth. Now that she knew when it had happened, she had to know the details. The day his mother had died, he'd had a gig at a bar in Alabama. She remembered how worried she'd been when she'd had to call him with the news. Because his feelings toward his mother were so conflicting, she hadn't been sure how he'd react. She'd thought he'd taken it well—or as well as anyone can take that kind of news. Apparently, she'd been wrong.

He glanced down at the blanket on his lap. Pulling off a piece of lint, he studiously rolled it between his fingers. "As I said, it was the night my mother died. When you called to tell me, something inside me snapped. I hung up the phone and looked around the bar I was working in, a seedy joint in a hick town. Suddenly I realized that I was the failure my mother had always claimed I was."

"You were never a failure!" Annie objected instantly.

He released a bitter laugh. "What would you have called me then? For God's sake, Annie. I was twenty-eight years old and I wasn't even making enough money to rent a decent apartment. If it hadn't been for you, I'd have probably been homeless."

"You were struggling, just like nearly every other musician does before they make it," she retorted defensively. "There's no shame in that, Tanner."

"No, there isn't any shame in that. Where the shame comes in is when you let your wife spend eight years of her life killing herself by working two jobs to support you while you run around chasing rainbows."

"I never complained."

"That's right. You never complained, and maybe that's why it took me so long to see that I had become like Peter Pan. I wasn't getting anywhere because you were indulging me in my fantasy. Because you were, I didn't need to grow up and take responsibility for myself and my wife."

"Are you saying you resented me?" she said with a gasp. She couldn't believe he would criticize her for doing everything in her power to make sure he fulfilled his dream.

"I told you there were going to be parts of this story that would hurt you and make you mad at me," he replied. "Are you sure you want to hear this?"

She paused for a split second, then declared, "Absolutely." She crossed her arms over her chest. As she did so, she decided there was a good possibility she was going to end up hating him.

"Okay. Just remember, you asked to hear it," he warned. When she didn't respond, he said, "I was furious with myself for being a failure. I was furious with you for helping me remain a failure. But most of all, I was furious with my mother for dying before I could prove to her that I wasn't one. At that moment I hated her, and I mean I truly hated her. So I did what any stupid fool would do under the circumstances. I got drunk."

"*You* got drunk?" Annie repeated, astounded. Of all the confessions he'd made so far, that was the one that truly shocked her. Because of his mother's drinking problem, she'd never seen him take so much as a sip of cough syrup containing alcohol.

"Hey, you know what my mother always said about me. The apple doesn't fall far from the tree."

"That's a bunch of bull and you know it."

He shrugged. "Maybe. All I know for sure is that I sat down at the bar and started drinking. It was a slow night, and I got to talking with the bartender, who happened to be a woman a few years older than me. She'd just gone through a particularly nasty divorce, so we swapped sob stories while I drowned my sorrows in beer. When the bar closed for the night, she invited me back to her place to try some whiskey that was supposedly out of this world. Since I was pretty much out of this world myself by then, I can't verify her claim. I can tell you, however, that we drained that bottle in record time, and when we were done, she was as smashed as I was."

"And then you went to bed together," Annie muttered dryly, coming to the natural conclusion.

He shrugged again. "To tell you the truth, I'm not sure when we went to bed, and if it helps at all, I don't even remember making love with her. All I do remember is waking up the next morning with a hangover that I was sure would kill me and a naked woman beside me. Since I was also naked and wearing a condom, I was pretty sure that we hadn't just been drinking buddies."

Annie frowned. "If you were wearing a condom, then how..."

He made a noise of disgust. "That was my first question, and believe me, I insisted on a blood test. I don't know what happened. Maybe it broke. Maybe I didn't put it on right. Hell, in the condition I was in, I was lucky to have used it in the first place."

He paused and stared at her intently as he said, "I'd never once cheated on you before that night, Annie, and I swear I've never cheated on you since. When she tracked me down a few months later and told me she was pregnant, I couldn't believe that I'd had such bad luck. One time—one lousy time that I couldn't even remember—and I got the woman pregnant."

"So after that night you came home to your wife, whom you happened to resent, and picked up as if nothing had happened," she summarized bitterly.

He sighed heavily. "Annie, my resentment toward you lasted as long as one drunken night. The next morning I realized that none of my problems were your fault, but old habits die hard. I was mad at myself, and it was easier to blame you than to feel guilty for everything I'd put you through. When I recognized that, I decided to give myself another six months to make it. After that, I was going to settle down, get a decent job and take care of you for a change.

"It was as if that decision made everything finally fall into place," he said. "Maybe it was my change in attitude, or maybe it was that I became more discerning about what jobs I took. Whatever it was, it worked, because shortly after that Daniel heard me sing and offered to take me on as a client. And, as you know, not long after that I landed the contract with NCR. The dream had finally come true, and I wasn't going to have to live off you any longer. I was finally a *man*, Annie. God, how I wish my mother could have lived just a few months longer so I could have made her eat her words," he finished harshly.

He was staring at some unseen point in space, and his expression was a combination of anger and despair. Annie's heart twisted, and she became furious with his mother for doing this to him. She wished there was something she could say to take his torment away, but she knew there wasn't, because his problem went back to the cradle.

She knew his mother had also dreamed of becoming a country-and-western star. Then she'd gotten involved with a musician and had ended up pregnant with Tanner. When the musician found out, he'd disappeared, leaving her alone, unmarried and stuck with the responsibility of raising a child. Annie had never figured out why she hadn't considered adoption, but she hadn't. When she'd had Tanner, she'd had to quit singing and get a regular job. She'd blamed Tanner for ruining her dream, and she'd never let him forget it. At the tender age of five he'd been so desperate for her love that he'd decided he would become a star, just like she had always dreamed *she* would. The unfortunate part was that Annie knew he didn't recognize his motivations. In his mind, becoming a star had been his dream and his alone. It was the only way he could cope.

Suddenly, he looked at her and said, "Well, now you know the entire story. I know it's bad, but I'm sure it isn't as bad as you thought it was."

He was right. It wasn't as bad as she'd thought. It was worse, because she recognized now that he'd never be able to defeat his demons, that he'd always be chasing an illusive dream. No matter what he did or how much he accomplished, it wouldn't be enough, because it would never give him what he wanted most—his mother's love.

She wanted to go to him, wrap her arms around him and take away his pain. She refrained from doing so, however, because she knew that the only person who could heal Tanner was Tanner himself. Although she wanted to believe that someday he would be able to do that, she wasn't sure it was true.

"Why didn't you tell me what had happened when you found out she was pregnant?" she asked.

He eyed her askance. "Because I knew you'd leave me, and I couldn't see losing you over a stupid mistake that wasn't really even my fault."

"A child is not a 'stupid mistake.' He's your *son!*" she declared, aghast at his attitude toward the boy.

He shook his head. "You're wrong, Annie. He's *her* son."

"No, Tanner," she corrected vehemently. "He's your son, too. You fathered him. You have a responsibility to him."

"I'm aware of that," he muttered, scowling at her. "Daniel sends his mother a support check every month, and has ever since I signed the contract with NCR."

"Daniel knew about this?"

"Of course he knew. How else was I going to send her money without you finding out?"

Annie wasn't sure what made her more angry—that Daniel had been involved in the conspiracy or that Tanner referred to his son as a "stupid mistake."

"You know, your mother was right," she blurted out. "The apple doesn't fall far from the tree, because you're just like your father."

The moment the words left her mouth, she wanted to snatch them back. His mother was an open wound for him, but his father, who had abandoned him before his birth, was a festering ulcer.

He got up off the sofa so fast that she didn't even see him move. One moment he'd been lying there, and the next he had a hand braced on either arm of her chair, his face mere inches from hers, as he snapped, "Don't you ever compare me to him! I don't come close to being the kind of bastard he was. At least I pay child support!"

Oddly enough, his expression was almost blank, but his voice held a deceptively soft tone that emphasized his fury. At any other time such intense wrath might have made Annie back down, but this time it lit her own temper.

She leaned forward so that their noses almost touched as she shot back, "You're right. You're worse than him, because at least your father had the decency to desert you. You could spend your childhood making up all the stories you wanted about why he had to leave. But what stories will your son be able to make up, Tanner? He'll know you send money. How do you think he's going to feel when he realizes his father just can't be bothered with him?

"How can you, of all people, do that to him?" she railed. "Don't you see that you're not only behaving like your father, but you're also acting like your mother? *You* made a mistake. But that child is going to pay for it, because I can guarantee that if he doesn't end up hating you just like you hate your father, he'll spend the rest of his life trying to find a way to make you love him. And, like what happened to you, nothing he does is going to get him that parental love, because you are just like your mother. You don't give a damn about him or anyone else. All you give a damn about is yourself and your blasted *dream!*"

As she spoke, his expression changed to one of un-mitigated rage. He pushed away from the chair, placed his hands on his hips and glared down at her. Again, his voice was frighteningly soft as he asked, "Are you through?"

She rose to her feet, forcing him to step back. Wrapping the blanket tightly around herself, she raised her chin haughtily and replied, "I was through eighteen months ago, Tanner. You're the one dragging this out."

With that, she turned and marched toward the stairs. When she was halfway up them, she stopped and turned back to face him, saying, "By the way, I want to thank you for forcing this confrontation, because you finally made me open my eyes. All those years I was married to you, I only had one dream. I wanted a baby—*your* baby. Now that I know just what kind of a man you are, I see that realizing that dream would have been the biggest mistake of my life. I'm also sure that you'll fall to your knees and thank your lucky stars to know that I miscarried one of your *stupid mistakes* the day I saw the picture of your son in the newspaper."

She didn't wait to see his reaction. She swung back around and continued up the stairs, ignoring the pain that was ripping her up inside. As she reached the top, she decided that first thing tomorrow morning she was leaving. If it ruined her career in Nashville, so be it. She'd rather be an accountant than ever have to see Tanner Thaddeus Chapel again.

TANNER COULDN'T THINK. He couldn't breathe. He couldn't even move. All he could do was watch Annie climb the stairs with all the regal bearing of a queen.

When she finally disappeared from sight, he closed his eyes and her voice reverberated in his ears. *I miscarried one of your stupid mistakes the day I saw the picture of your son in the newspaper.*

Now he understood why the child had been such a big deal for her. *Dear God in heaven, she had had a miscarriage, and he hadn't even known she was pregnant!*

Even worse, she'd miscarried the day she'd found out about his one idiotic night of drunken self-pity. Why hadn't she told him she was pregnant? And, for God's sake, when she'd lost the baby, why hadn't she come to him? Why had she dealt with the loss on her own?

Because that's what she did throughout your entire marriage. She shouldered the burdens so you could chase after rainbows.

That truth hurt so badly that he thought the pain might kill him. What made it even more unbearable was the realization that while she'd been trying to grapple with the loss of her baby, he'd been fighting the divorce tooth and nail. My God, he'd even filed for custody of her cat, the only thing she had left to love!

Fury at himself surged through him with such force that if the wall hadn't been made of logs, he would have started punching holes in it. He still considered giving it a few good jabs, but even as he clenched his hands into fists, he knew that it wasn't going to help. No amount of physical pain was going to ease his guilt.

Suddenly, he recalled just how much Annie had wanted a baby, and he realized that even if she hadn't had a miscarriage, the fact that he'd fathered a child would have devastated her. They'd put off having a family because of their financial circumstances, but every now and then she had come home with some cute little toy or article of baby clothing that she'd found on sale somewhere. Then she'd carefully pack it away until the day arrived when her own dream would finally come true. How could he possibly have forgotten that?

He violently thrust a hand through his hair as her voice again reverberated in his ears. *You're just like your mother. All you give a damn about is yourself and your blasted dream!*

Was he really that selfish? That callous? Did he, like his mother, have some warped place in his soul?

He wanted to answer with a resounding no. What he came up with was a hesitant maybe. He refused to answer yes because, unlike his mother, he knew he was capable of love. Indeed, he loved Annie so much that sometimes just the immeasurable dimensions of his feelings for her overwhelmed him. From the very first moment he'd seen her, she'd touched him deep inside where no one had ever touched him before or since. Then he'd met her, and he'd fallen instantly and hopelessly in love. She'd not only been good and kind and gentle, but she had believed in him without question and had never allowed him to doubt himself. Without her, he'd probably have ended up like his mother—a bitter drunk stumbling from bar stool to bar stool while bemoaning the loss of his dream.

So how had he paid her back for all she'd done for him? He'd killed the only thing that she had ever wanted from him. He'd destroyed her dream, and he was so ashamed of himself that he wanted to die.

He hadn't really cried since he was five years old, but he wanted to wail as Annie had done tonight. He knew he couldn't allow himself that purging of grief, though, because his crimes against her were too horrible to be forgiven. It was only fair that he carry around this soul-crushing remorse for the rest of his life.

So instead of indulging himself in tears, he limped to the door. Each step sent an agonizing pain through his knee, which had been damaged even further when he'd leapt off the sofa at Annie's declaration that he was just like his father. Now he realized she was right. Like it or not, the child he'd fathered was a part of him, so why didn't he feel anything toward him? Why couldn't he dredge up enough decency to at least make an effort to be a dad? Was it some kind of genetic weakness?

Pushing open the door, he stepped onto the porch, lifted his face skyward and let the icy rain batter him. Yes, he was as worthless as his father and as soulless as his mother. The worst part was he didn't know how to change that and wasn't sure that he could if he did know how. Like they'd both admitted, the apple didn't fall far from the tree.

As he stared into the darkness, Tanner considered taking a long walk in the woods. He could get lost, freeze to death, and then he'd never be able to hurt Annie again.

But as much as the thought appealed to him, he knew he couldn't do that to her. She would be the one who'd suffer, because he knew her well enough to know that if anything happened to him, she'd blame herself. He'd already caused her enough heartache. He sure wasn't going to make her spend the rest of her life condemning herself for his death.

So instead of taking a suicidal walk in the woods, he went back inside and headed for the music room, oblivious of the cold and his drenched clothing. All he knew was that he had to do what he always did when he was faced with seething, painful emotions. He had to turn them into music.

As he sat down with his guitar, he expected that the melody he composed would be discordant, even brutal. But what emerged was something so exquisitely beautiful that it brought a lump to his throat. Never had his music affected him so deeply, so profoundly. It thrust its way into his soul, turning him inside out and upside down. But, like all his other melodies, he didn't know what it was trying to tell him, and without Annie, he never would.

When he'd finished the last note, he set the guitar aside, propped his elbows on his knees and buried his face in his hands. After what had occurred between him and Annie tonight, he knew that, first thing in the morning, she would leave. He had to decide if he was going to do the honorable thing and let her go, or if he was going to be the despicable, selfish bastard he was and fight to win her back.

9

THE ROOM WAS SO bitterly cold that Annie didn't want to get out of bed. Evidently the power had been off all night, because even fully clothed, with half a dozen thermal blankets and a down comforter piled on top of her, she was shivering. Just the thought of throwing back the covers made her teeth chatter.

But it isn't the cold keeping you in bed, she chided herself. *It's that you don't want to face Tanner.*

She let out a heartfelt groan. After the bombshell she'd dropped on him, he would certainly think they had a lot more to talk about. That's why she hated confrontations and avoided them whenever possible. Too often things were said in anger that should never have been said at all, and then you had to deal with the aftermath.

But by avoiding a discussion, aren't you behaving just like Tanner? Aren't you refusing to acknowledge your problems and deal with them?

With another groan, she buried her face in her pillow. As much as she wanted to deny it, she knew her conscience was right. In some ways, she was just as culpable as he was. She should have confronted him eighteen months ago and gotten everything out in the open, but she'd chosen to keep the miscarriage a secret instead. So why, after all this time, had she told him about it? Why hadn't she just kept her mouth shut?

Because it was difficult enough for her to deal with the fact that another woman had his baby and her own baby was gone. To realize that he didn't appear to have any feelings toward the boy had been more than she could handle. As ignoble as it was, she'd wanted him to hurt as badly as she was hurting. She'd wanted him to suffer as she was suffering. She knew it was convoluted thinking, but she'd felt that by rejecting his son, he'd also been rejecting the child she'd lost, and she'd wanted to punish him for that.

Now, in the morning light, she recognized that they were dealing with two entirely different situations, and in some ways she could understand his indifference toward his son. It wasn't as if he and the boy's mother had been intimately acquainted, so there was nothing there on which to base an emotional attachment to the child they shared. She and Tanner, on the other hand, had had years of emotional bonding. She supposed that's where the rub came in. Though she wanted to believe that he would have felt differently about their child, there was a nagging part of her that couldn't help wondering if he would have. He was so focused on chasing after a dream he couldn't fulfill that he didn't have anything left to give to anyone else.

Intuition told her that the only way he could come to grips with his past was to learn to give of himself, and the best place for him to start doing that was with his son. Perhaps if he gave the child the love and nurturing his own parents had never given him, he might begin to see his dream for what it really was—a frantic search for parental love that could never be won.

Instead of railing at him last night, she should have calmly pointed out her insights. It might not have made a difference, but at least he would have had a chance to think about it. Now he would never do that, because she'd forced him into a defensive posture. Instead of analyzing his own motivations, he'd probably spent all night stewing about what she'd blurted out. And she had no doubt he was waiting to grill her about it.

"I never should have come here," she mumbled, rolling to her back and staring gloomily at the ceiling. "I knew in my heart that something like this would happen."

But she had come, and now she was going to have to deal with Tanner's reaction.

"Well, look at it this way," she said as she forced herself to throw back the covers, shivering when the cold air swept over her. "One more bout with Tanner and you'll be at the end of this chapter of your life. Then you can begin a new one, and, hopefully, it will have a better ending."

Sitting up, she rubbed her hands over her eyes, which were still so swollen from her crying session that she was surprised she could see. As she dragged her fingers through her tangled hair, she surveyed her clothes. They looked as if they'd been slept in, which, of course, they had.

She gave a rueful shake of her head. When she'd made her dramatic exit last night she'd forgotten that her suitcase and purse were still downstairs. Now she would have to have her final showdown with Tanner looking like something Pooh wouldn't drag in. She was vain enough not to want this to be the way he remembered her, but there wasn't much she could do about it.

With another sigh, she slid her feet into her shoes and stood up. She'd make a quick trip to the bathroom and wash her face. Then she'd get this over with and head for home.

When she opened the door, however, she froze in her tracks. Evidently she wasn't even going to get to wash her face, because Tanner was sitting on the floor across from her room, his legs stretched out in front of him and his back against the wall.

Her gaze automatically swept over him. Though she hadn't yet looked in the mirror, she suspected that she couldn't look much worse than him. His hair was standing on end, as though he'd run his hands through it continuously. His clothes were as wrinkled as hers. His eyes were bloodshot, and his weary expression suggested that he hadn't slept any better than she had. He also hadn't shaved, and the stubble of beard emphasized his disheveled appearance and his pallor.

When he suddenly shivered violently, Annie realized he was still wearing nothing more than a T-shirt and denims. Since she was practically frostbitten in her sweater, she figured he must be frozen solid, particularly since she suspected he'd been sitting there for quite some time.

"Good heavens, Tanner, what is wrong with you?" she asked impatiently. "You should be down in front of the fire instead of sitting up here in the cold. You're liable to catch pneumonia, or worse, get laryngitis, and that could damage your vocal chords. Don't you have any common sense?"

Tanner stared at Annie in disbelief. Her hair was a wild tangle. Her eyes were not only almost swollen shut, but the dark bruises beneath them made her look like a refugee from a war zone. It was obvious she'd had as bad a night as he had, and after all he'd put her through, she should be screaming invectives at him. Instead, the first words out of her mouth were concern for him!

"I don't believe you," he said. "You're the one who's been to hell and back, and instead of worrying about yourself, you're fussing over me. Don't you have one selfish bone in your body?"

She gave him a wary look as she crossed her arms in front of her and slipped her hands up the sleeves of her sweater. "Actually, I have two selfish bones, maybe even three."

He regarded her dubiously. "You don't know how much I'd like to believe that."

"Believe it," she stated dryly. "I am not a saint."

He drew his good leg up and rested his arm on his knee. "I wouldn't be so sure about that." When she didn't respond, he stared at her searchingly before murmuring, "Why didn't you tell me about the baby? I know you were angry with me, but didn't you think I had a right to know? It was my baby, too, Annie. I should have known."

Annie closed her eyes and leaned heavily against the doorjamb. She'd known the question was inevitable, but she hadn't expected him to sound so plaintive. Why couldn't he be angry, or even dispassionate? She could handle those two emotions, but she couldn't handle him being mournful. It was too close to her own raw feelings.

Though she would have liked nothing better than to run downstairs and out the door so she wouldn't have to talk about this, she knew she couldn't. She'd opened this can of worms, and he deserved to have his questions answered, even if it did tear her to shreds to talk about it.

With an inward sigh of resignation, she opened her eyes and said, "Since you didn't know I was pregnant in the first place, it didn't seem fair to tell you about the miscarriage."

"Fair?" he repeated in quiet incredulity. "Dear God, Annie, you'd just learned that I had cheated on you, and when you did, you lost your baby. After all that, you were worried about being *fair* to me?"

"Yes, I was," she answered. "Outside of being just plain mean, what would telling you have accomplished?"

"I could have been there for you."

"I didn't want you there."

It wasn't her words that cut Tanner to the bone. It was her unemotional tone. It told him that she'd moved beyond the realm of caring—of feeling. And he knew at that moment that he'd lost her forever.

His expression must have revealed his pain, because Annie suddenly said, "I'm sorry, Tanner. I didn't mean to hurt you. I was just telling you the truth."

"I know." Though he knew he should drop the subject, he couldn't stop himself from asking, "How long had you known you were pregnant, and why didn't you tell me?"

She shrugged uneasily and glanced down at the floor. "You had just left for Europe when I found out, and it wasn't the kind of news I wanted to tell you over the telephone. I was saving it as a welcome-home surprise."

Tanner wouldn't have believed that anything could make him hurt worse than he was already hurting, but that simple confession completely unraveled him. He could just see her holding the secret close to her heart while making plans to spring the news on him when he came home. Knowing her as well as he did, he was sure she'd planned the entire scene right down to the smallest detail. She must have been so excited, and then she'd made a trip to the grocery store and seen the story about his "affair" plastered across the front pages of the tabloids. No wonder she hated him. At that moment, he hated himself.

"I'm so sorry I made you lose the baby, Annie."

"You didn't make me lose it, Tanner, and I'm sorry I made you feel as if you did," Annie whispered hoarsely, tears welling into her eyes again at the tortured look he gave her. She understood the guilt he was grappling with right now. She'd been battling it for a year and a half, and only in the last few months had she begun to reach the point where she could stop blaming herself. "It's true that seeing that picture of your son was a shock, but the doctor said it probably would have happened anyway."

It was the word *probably* that reverberated in Tanner's ears. If she hadn't seen that newspaper article, maybe...

"Oh, God, why did I do it?" he said with a groan. "If I just hadn't started drinking that night. If I could just go back in time!"

"Don't do this to yourself, Tanner," Annie replied, barely able to speak around the lump in her throat. Last night she'd wanted him to hurt, but now, watching him do so, she couldn't bear it. "Believe me, all the recriminations in the world aren't going to change anything. They're only going to eat you up inside until you can't stand it. All you can do is accept that it just wasn't meant to be, and in time, you'll even start believing it."

He closed his eyes and rested his head against the wall for a long time. When he finally opened them, there were tears shimmering in them, and Annie felt as if the world had just dropped out from under her. She'd never seen Tanner cry. Never!

Oh, God, what have I done? she moaned inwardly, tears again welling into her own eyes. His grief was so intense, so alive, that it struck a resonating chord deep inside her. She wrapped her arms around her middle in an effort to stem her own agony. She wanted to slide to the floor and burst into sobs, but she knew from experience that it would only make the pain worse.

Instead, she took several deep, calming breaths. When she was sure she had herself under control, she said, "I'm sorry, Tanner. I didn't mean to hurt you like this."

"Why not?" he asked bitterly. "It's what I deserve after what I did to you. And *I'm* sorry, Annie. Truly sorry. About the baby and everything else I've done to you. All you ever did was love me, and I can't believe I've treated you so badly. I'd give anything to be able to go back and change it all, but I can't. Since I can't, I'm going to do the next best thing."

"What's that?" she asked warily as he began to push himself to his feet.

He waited until he was standing before announcing, "I'm leaving."

She blinked at him in confusion. "Leaving?"

He nodded. "According to the weather forecast, this ice storm is going to hang around for two or three days.

I know that if I don't leave, you will, and I don't want you risking your life out there on icy roads."

Before she could object, he continued, "The refrigerator and cupboards are fully stocked, and I spoke to the utility company a little while ago. They assured me the power will be on in another hour or two, but even if it isn't, there's plenty of wood for the fireplace. You'll be okay until the weather clears."

Annie was so stunned by this unforeseen turn of events that she could only stare at him in bewilderment when he gave her a heartbreakingly sad smile and said, "Goodbye, Annie. Have the wonderful life you deserve. I promise, I'll never bother you again."

As she watched him turn and limp away, an inexplicable feeling of panic rose inside her. This wasn't the way things were supposed to be happening! Tanner was supposed to be acting like an irrational jerk, not like a sensible, reasonable guy. For pity's sake, he had never been reasonable a single day in his life! He was supposed to yell at her for keeping the truth from him. She was supposed to yell back at him for putting her in such a position. Then she could grab Pooh and her suitcase and storm out in righteous indignation, resolved never to see him again. For it to end any other way was—was . . . She didn't know what it was, but it wasn't supposed to be like this!

Just let him go, an inner voice urged. *It doesn't matter how it ends, only that it's finally over.*

Rationally, Annie knew that the voice was right, but irrationally, she was furious with Tanner for doing this to her. How dare he just say goodbye and wish her a wonderful life? Who did he think he was—some country-and-western parody of Sir Galahad? Well, he was *not* going to do this to her! After all he'd put her through, he owed her, and she was going to collect her due in full!

TANNER HAD JUST REACHED the stairs when Annie ordered, "You just stop right there, Tanner Chapel."

Her quiet but angry tone startled him, and he turned to look at her in confusion. "What's wrong?"

"What's wrong?" she repeated as she scowled at him. "Well, for one thing, what about your album? If you think I'm going to have Roy fire me because—"

"Annie, don't be silly," he interrupted soothingly when he understood the cause of her distress. It dismayed him to realize she'd think he could be that cruel, but he also recognized that he hadn't given her much reason to believe otherwise. "As soon as I get back to Nashville, I'll call Roy and tell him we can't work together. I'll make sure he understands that this is my decision, so you won't have a hassle from him. I promise."

If he'd been confused before, he was downright baffled when she shot back, "And what if that isn't what *I* want?"

"Of course it's what you want."

"I can't believe you have the nerve to stand there and tell me what I want. You can't read my mind!"

As she spoke, she perched her hands on her hips. It was a sure sign that her temper was escalating, and for the life of him, he couldn't figure out why. "Annie, you're not making any sense."

"I happen to be making perfect sense," she retorted. "You're the one that's having the reasoning problem. You're feeling guilty, so you've decided to be noble by plopping your Stetson on your head, grabbing your guitar and driving off into an ice storm. Not only is that stupid, it's dangerous, but that's okay, because you're not a *frail little woman* like me. You're the big he-man who can take care of himself—even if you can barely walk—so far be it from me to interfere with your thriving machismo.

"However, I have a career to think about," she went on, "and my best opportunity for success is to write the lyrics for your new album. So if you think you're going to walk out that door and jeopardize my career by getting yourself killed, you'd better think again. You're going to stay, and *we're* going to complete those songs. Once they're finished, you can be as noble as you want and do any dangerous, stupid thing you desire. But until those songs are finished, your butt is mine. Have you got that?"

He shook his head. "I don't think it's a good idea for me to stay."

She lifted her chin an unyielding notch. "I didn't ask you what you thought, Tanner. I told you what you're going to do, and I'm not going to take no for an answer."

Her stubborn expression told him she meant what she said, and Tanner felt torn. She had a valid point about her career, and after everything he'd done to her, he knew he owed her this much. But for once in his life he was trying to do the right thing by her, and it had taken him most of the night to overcome his selfish need to hold on to her. He wanted to believe that if he stayed, he'd have enough moral fiber to let her go when the time came. He knew in his heart, however, that he wouldn't. When it came to her, he was weak and always would be.

"Look, there's a simple solution to this problem," he stated, suddenly realizing that there was a compromise that would let them both have what they want. "You've already got notes on all the melodies, and I trust your instincts. I'll give you back your copy of the tape, and you can write the lyrics from it."

The moment the words left his mouth, Tanner realized he'd just confessed to taking her tape, and he wanted to curse himself for his stupidity. Even as he began to hope that she hadn't picked up on his slip of the tongue, she asked suspiciously, "What do you mean, you'll give me back my copy of the tape?"

"What I meant was that I'll send you another copy of the tape," he quickly improvised.

"Why would I need another copy?" she countered, sounding even more suspicious. "I have a copy at home."

Damn! He'd dug himself in deeper, and he didn't know how to answer. And then he didn't need to answer, because she suddenly exclaimed, "You took my tape, didn't you?"

He opened his mouth to deny her accusation, but he knew that lying to her would just make the situation worse. With a resigned sigh, he muttered, "Yes, I took it."

"Why?" she demanded in outrage.

He shot her a chagrined look. "It doesn't matter why, Annie. I'll give it back to you, and—"

"Why did you take it?" she broke in stubbornly.

He rubbed a hand against his whiskered jaw as he sought some reasonable excuse to explain his actions. Unfortunately, his mind wasn't cooperating, and he concluded that the best answer was to just tell her the truth—or at least a condensed version of it. "I was afraid you'd get the songs written too fast."

"What are you saying? That you were afraid I'd do sloppy work?" she cried indignantly.

"Of course not!"

"Then why did you take the tape?"

"I already told you it doesn't matter why. What matters is that I'm giving it back to you. You can write the lyrics, and we'll both have what we want, okay?"

"No, it isn't okay!" she railed, jabbing a finger in his direction. "You gaslighted me by making me think I'd left the tape at home, and I want to know why."

By now she was glaring at him so murderously that Tanner was surprised he didn't burst into flame. He decided that he might as well confess everything. Once she knew the whole story, she'd be more than willing to let him leave.

Stuffing his hands into his back pockets, he warned, "All right, if you really want to know why I did it, I'll tell you, but you aren't going to like it." When her only response was to continue to glare at him, he said, "I stole the tape because I wanted more time with you so I could win you back."

Her mouth dropped open and she stared at him in shock. After several seconds passed, she closed her mouth, then declared, "That's crazy. We're divorced."

"We may be divorced, but I've never stopped loving you."

"Don't say that!"

"Why not? It's the truth."

"Dammit, Tanner," she frantically whispered, "I don't want to hear this!"

"I'm sure you don't," he agreed sadly, "but that doesn't change my feelings. Ever since you left me, I've been lost. I can't sleep through the night. I have to force myself to eat. Even work doesn't fill the void. If anything, it makes it worse, because I know that when the performance is over, you'll still be gone.

"I was—no, I *am*—desperate," he continued, unable to stop the words now that he'd started speaking. "I was hoping that if we came up here, we could recapture what we used to have and I could make you fall in love with me again. Now I understand that I hurt you so badly you'll never be able to forgive me. But even though I know that, I also realize that if I stay I won't be able to leave you alone. I want you and need you too badly, Annie, and I'm just not strong enough to stay here with you and do the right thing."

She opened her mouth to reply, but he held up his hand. "The tape's in the vase on the mantel—the one with the silk flowers in it. When you get the lyrics written, just give them to Roy. I hope every one of the songs is a hit, and that your career goes right through the ceiling. You deserve the best of everything, Annie. I'm just sorry you wasted so many years of your life on a loser like me."

With that, he turned again and started down the stairs, knowing he couldn't continue this discussion with her. If he did, he'd probably end up dropping to his knees, sprain and all, and begging her to give him a second chance. If she said no, it would kill him, but even more frightening was the thought that she might say yes. If she did give him another chance, he'd probably blow it, and the thought of having to lose her all over again was too horrible to even think about.

When he reached the bottom of the stairs, he didn't bother to stop for his suitcase, knowing that even that slight delay might be enough to make him change his mind. He and Annie were over, and he had to make sure it stayed that way. It was the right thing—the only thing—to do.

BEFORE ANNIE COULD assimilate even half of Tanner's confession, he turned and disappeared down the stairs. She stood staring into space while her mind screamed, *He loves me!*

But even as hope began to stir inside her, the voice of reason whispered, *Even if he does love you, it isn't the right kind of love. You need more than dreams, and that's all he has to offer.*

But now you understand why he's the way he is, and with your help he could change, her heart challenged. *He says he loves you, and you know you still love him, so don't you owe yourself another chance to at least see if it can work?*

With a groan, she buried her face in her hands. She knew that the only sensible thing to do was let him go. He was right. He'd hurt her too badly, and she didn't know if she could forgive him. And even if she could, it wouldn't solve the major problem that had existed between them, because he would still be a star. He'd still have the crowds swarming over him and the cameras trained on him. He'd still have the women flirting with him, and she'd still feel inadequate.

But there would be one difference. She'd no longer feel completely worthless, because she now had a career and her own sense of identity. And because she did have those things, wasn't it possible that they could resolve all the other issues and come to a compromise that would make them both happy?

Even as she again felt hope stirring inside her, she squashed it. There was one issue she wasn't sure she could ever reconcile, and that was his son. In order for Tanner to come to grips with his past, he had to develop a relationship with the boy. If he did, the child would become an integral part of his life.

Could she deal with that? Could she look at that little boy and not be reminded of her own loss? Could she accept him into her life and not resent him, possibly even grow to hate him, because of his very existence?

She wanted to believe that she was mature enough to never blame a child for his parents' sins, but as she'd told Tanner earlier, she was not a saint. Just the thought of having to see the child, talk to him, caused a snarl of emotions too tangled to unravel, because those were things she'd never be able to do with her own baby.

Her head shot up when she heard the front door slam, and her heart began to beat in a frenzied rhythm. Tanner was leaving, which meant she had to make a decision, and she had to make it now.

Her instincts for self-preservation began screaming at her to let him go, telling her that if she gave him another chance, he'd probably end up hurting her again. She'd barely survived losing him the first time. She didn't think she could do it again.

"Oh, God, what should I do?" she prayed frantically when she heard his car start.

Unfortunately, no answer came from on high, and though she still didn't know what she wanted, she did know that she couldn't let him go until she had reached a decision.

She ran toward the stairs and bounded down them two at a time. Then she raced to the front door and threw it open, screaming, "Tanner!"

But even as she yelled his name, she realized it was too late. His car was gone.

10

TANNER CURSED and slammed his fist against the steering wheel. He'd no more than turned off the long, winding drive from the cabin when his car had gone into a skid. Now its front end was sitting in the ditch along the road, and he didn't have to put the wheels into reverse to know he was stuck. That meant he was going to have to hike back to the cabin and call a tow truck. Since the cabin was out in the middle of nowhere and the weather was so bad, he doubted anyone would come up here until the storm cleared. And that meant he was going to have to spend at least another day and night with Annie.

Why were the Fates doing this to him? he wondered morosely as he stared out into the rain, which was coming down so hard that it sounded like hail against the car roof. It had been difficult enough for him to stay away from Annie. If he went back, it would be next to impossible. It just wasn't fair!

But what else was new? Not much in his life had been fair. The only thing he hadn't had to struggle for was Annie's love, and maybe that was why he'd screwed up so badly with her. It had just come too damn easy. With another curse, he reached for the door handle, knowing that he might as well accept the inevitable and head back to the cabin.

He'd just climbed out when he heard a car coming, and his spirits rose. Maybe he wouldn't have to go back. Maybe he could hitch a ride to the small town at the foot of the mountain. But then he realized the car wasn't on the road but was coming from the direction of the cabin.

As he watched Annie's car come around the bend and instantly go into a skid, his eyes widened in horror. She wasn't headed for the ditch, but for the cliff on the other side of the road!

"No!" he bellowed as her car slid past him, and he started running after it. Too late, he realized his cowboy boots were not made for traversing ice. They lost traction on the frozen pavement and his feet shot out from under him. He landed on his back so hard that it knocked the breath out of him. Stunned, he could only lie there gasping, while fearfully listening for the crash of Annie's car going over the cliff.

But instead of hearing a crash, he heard the slam of a car door. A second later, Annie was kneeling beside him, a look of anxiety on her face as she gasped, "Tanner, are you okay?"

He was so relieved to see she was all right that he couldn't answer. As he watched the rain plaster her hair to her head, his love for her mushroomed inside his chest until it was a torturous ache. He wanted to grab her and hold her and never let her go. He wanted to kiss her and—

His wistful musing was interrupted by Annie demanding, "Tanner, answer me! Are you okay?"

"Yeah." He pushed himself up on his forearms and a wave of dizziness assaulted him. But the condition wasn't the result of a physical injury, it was caused by the sight of Annie's car resting sideways in the road, her back tires mere inches from the edge of the cliff. At the realization of just how close he'd come to losing her, fear exploded inside him with the same intensity that his love for her had only moments before. On the heels of that fear came an inexplicable rage.

He snapped his head toward her and bellowed, "Dammit, Annie! What the hell are you doing out in this storm? You almost killed yourself!"

She sat back on her heels. "I almost killed *myself*? *You're* the one lying flat on your back in the middle of the road!"

"That's because you were about to go over the cliff, and I was running after you!"

"Well, that's the most stupid thing I ever heard! What were you going to do? Grab my bumper and play Superman?"

Even as mad as he was, he recognized the absurdity of his actions. That only made him more furious. Sitting up, he said, "You didn't answer my question. What are you doing out here? I told you to stay at the cabin!"

Her spine stiffened and her eyes shot daggers at him. "Well, I know that this may come as a big surprise to you, but I don't have to do every blasted thing you tell me to do!"

"The hell you don't!" he roared, instinctively making a grab for her.

She was faster than him, and she shot to her feet. As she took several quick steps backward so that she was out of his reach, she threw her arms into the air and railed, "I don't know why I came chasing after you! You are the most obnoxious, arrogant, chauvinistic fool I've ever met, and for the life of me, I can't figure out why I'm still in love with you!"

Her mouth dropped open at the same time his did. As their eyes locked, she shook her head and began to back even farther away from him, as though distance would help her deny what she'd just said. But no amount of denial would ever erase the words from Tanner's mind. *She'd been coming after him. She was still in love with him!*

As he began to climb to his feet, he told himself that as much as he wanted to run to her, grab her and make her say the words again, he had to take this slowly. She may have said she loved him, but he recognized that accidentally blurting out her feelings was a far cry from dealing with them. There was now, however, a reason to hope, and he would cling to that with all the fervency of a drowning man clutching at a life preserver.

By the time he was standing, Annie had halted her retreat, but she stood poised with the alertness of a wild animal sensing danger. He knew that one false move on his part would send her running, and since his car was stuck in the ditch, he wasn't about to let that happen.

In an effort to ease the tension between them, he stuffed his hands into his back pockets and let his gaze flick over her. The rain had soaked her clothes, and both her sweater and her jeans clung to her slender body. Her hair was now a dripping mop, and even though there was a good ten feet between them, he could see that she was shivering uncontrollably.

As he returned his gaze to her face, he said in a conversational tone, "You're starting to turn blue, Annie. You should get back to the cabin before you freeze to death."

Annie blinked in confusion. She'd just admitted that she was still in love with him, and all he had to say was that she was turning blue? She couldn't decide whether she should be indignant or relieved. She'd certainly had no intention of exposing her feelings to him, but since she had, she expected some reaction other than an observation about her skin color! What was wrong with him? Hadn't he heard what she said?

She opened her mouth to speak, then closed it. She wasn't about to repeat her declaration of love, and she didn't know what else to say.

Thankfully, Tanner solved her dilemma by stating, "I'm serious, Annie. You need to get back to the cabin or you're going to end up sick."

"And what are you going to do?" she countered.

He shrugged. "What do you want me to do?"

Annie knew it was a loaded question. He was asking her to make a decision about him. If she asked him to stay, she'd be insinuating that there was a chance for them to reconcile, and she wasn't sure that was true. If, however, she asked him to go, she'd be saying it was over between them, and she wasn't ready to take that final step just yet, either.

She decided to compromise by saying, "I want you to come back to the cabin. We're not finished with the songs, and I think it would be better if we worked on them together."

"The songs are the only reason you want me to come back?"

"Dammit, Tanner! Why are you making this so difficult?"

"Because I want to know exactly where I stand," he answered. "I'll come back to the cabin and work on the songs with you, but only if it means you're going to give me—*us*—a chance. If you're not, then I need to know that right now."

"It isn't that simple!" she cried, balling her fingers into fists in frustration. "I've just spent a year and a half making myself forget you. You can't expect me to do a complete about-face in twenty-four hours!"

"I didn't say it was simple," he responded. "And I'm not asking you to do a complete about-face. All I want to know is where I stand at this very minute. Is there even a remote chance for us?"

Was there a remote chance for them? Annie asked herself. Though she wanted to believe there was, she still had her doubts. If she could just have some indication that he could change, that he could put his priorities in order, then maybe, just maybe, they could work things out. But there was nothing to help her make that decision.

Or was there? she wondered, suddenly recalling his new music. One of the reasons she hadn't recognized that he was the composer was because it was so different from anything he'd ever written. It had a texture and depth that he'd never displayed before, and the reason it had affected her so deeply was that she'd felt as if he had delved inside her and suffered heartbreak right along with her. Had their breakup hurt him as badly as it had her? Was it possible that his music was a true reflection of his feelings?

It dawned on her that it was not only possible, but entirely probable. She'd always understood that one of the reasons his music was so good was that he poured his emotions into it. But because of his horrible childhood, his feelings had always been too painful for him to face undiluted. She'd always had to put them into perspective for him, softening the blows and building on the good things, which was why she had to write his lyrics for him. She knew what he was truly feeling even when he didn't.

It was a shocking revelation that sent her mind reeling. No wonder his priorities were so screwed up! If he didn't know what he was feeling, then he couldn't know what he wanted. And if he didn't know what he wanted, then he couldn't make the right decisions. Why hadn't she seen that before?

Because she'd been so head over heels in love with him that she'd done everything for him, even *feel* for him. Since she'd been telling him what he felt, he hadn't learned to analyze his own feelings. That didn't, of course, excuse him for what he'd done to her, she acknowledged. Whether or not he was capable of analyzing his feelings, he did know the difference between right and wrong. And drinking himself into such a stupor that he didn't know what he was doing was definitely wrong. But she could now understand the emotional confusion he must have faced when he'd learned of his mother's death. Because she hadn't been there to help him understand his feelings, he'd simply reacted.

That was another shocking revelation. Indeed, she was so stunned that the world seemed to tilt for a moment. She'd been blaming him for everything, but she was the one who had fostered his emotional dependence on her. So, in some ways, she was just as responsible for what had happened as he was.

Annie focused her eyes on Tanner and extended her hand toward him. "Let's go home."

Tanner realized that this was her way of saying she was willing to give him another chance, and though it was the answer to his prayers, it made him uneasy. He searched her face, looking for something to explain his apprehension, but she looked so serene that her expression was almost angelic.

And that was what was wrong, he finally concluded grimly. She was too calm, and he'd learned ages ago that he'd much rather deal with an angry Annie than a placid one. When she was cool and composed, he never knew what she was thinking, and at this stage of the game, it was important that he know her thoughts at all times. Otherwise, he could end up blowing it without even realizing he was doing so.

So, instead of going to her and taking her proffered hand, he stuffed his hands deeper into his back pockets and said, "You're going to give me another chance just like that? No arguments? No histrionics? Just a simple, 'Let's go home'?"

She arched a brow. "Isn't that enough?"

He shook his head. "Nope."

"What do you mean, 'nope'?" she demanded, her hands automatically flying to her hips.

He barely bit back his triumphant grin. *This* was the Annie he was could deal with. "It means it's not enough. I want to know why you're doing it."

She brushed a hand over her wet head in agitation. "Tanner, in case you haven't noticed, we're out in an ice storm. Can't this conversation wait until we're back at the cabin?"

He shook his head again. "I know you too well, Annie. Once we're back at the cabin, you'll find a million excuses to put off talking about it. That means I'll end up walking around on eggshells, terrified that at any moment I'm going to say or do something that will explode in my face. I want another chance with you, and I'll do whatever it takes to get it. All I ask in return is that you be honest with me and tell me why you've decided to do this."

Annie stared at him in disbelief. He'd done everything but get down on his knees and beg her for another chance. Now that she was giving him one, he was demanding an explanation?

That made her so mad she wanted to scream, though she couldn't decide if she was irritated at him for being so ridiculous or at herself for loving him despite his foolishness. The worst part was, she knew exactly what he wanted from her. She'd accidentally confessed that she still loved him, and his ego wanted to hear the words again. Well, he could stuff his ego up his Stetson. She was not going to spurt avowals of love at his every whim!

"You're nuts, Tanner! Absolutely bats-in-the-belfry certifiable!" she declared.

"If that's true, then why are you giving me another chance?" he taunted.

"Because, idiot that I am, I care about you. If that's not a good enough reason for you, then forget it, because I am not going to stand out here in the freezing cold any longer. If you're coming back to the cabin with me, you have five seconds to get in the car. If you're not coming back, well, have a good life!"

Tanner scowled as she stormed toward the driver's side of her car. What did she mean, she was giving him another chance because she *cared* about him? Less than ten minutes ago she'd said she *loved* him! What was this *care* business?

When she started the car and put it into gear, he realized she was serious. If he didn't get in there pronto, she was going to leave him behind. With a curse, he started limping toward the car, deciding that he could wait until they got to the cabin to get this straightened out, after all. And he would get it straightened out. She was in *love* with him, not in *care* with him!

"THANK HEAVENS, the power's back on," Annie said as they walked in the front door, "and since the water heater's gas, there should be plenty of hot water. I'm going upstairs to take a shower. While I'm doing that, you can take one down here. I'll get you a change of clothes. Just put on your robe when you're done. I'll rewrap your knee when I bring your clothes down."

While she talked, she was heading for the stairs, and Tanner frowned. He hadn't been able to get her to say two words in the car, and now she was issuing orders like a general.

No, more like a mother, he grumbled to himself as he headed for the bathroom. He knew she was irked with him, and he'd much rather have her sniping at him than ignoring him as she had in the car. But insinuating that he was childish was taking things a bit too far. He was a man, not a child. Maybe it was time he reminded her just how much of a man he was.

By the time he climbed into the shower, the idea had become particularly appealing. Indeed, the more he thought about it, the more he realized that a little seduction was in order. She did, after all, *care* about him, and she had agreed to give them another chance.

Of course, he couldn't come on too strong, he cautioned himself. In the mood she was in, she'd probably bean him with something, at the very least. At the worst, she might change her mind and hightail it out the door. He wasn't about to risk losing her just to make a point. So, whatever he did, it had to seem innocent and casual—one of those man-woman things that just happen. Then, when her guard was down, he'd pounce.

"DAMMIT, TANNER. You did remember to bring clean underwear, didn't you?" Annie grumbled to herself as she searched the chest of drawers in the master bedroom.

So far she'd found about a half-dozen pairs of jeans and a dozen T-shirts, but there wasn't a pair of socks or undershorts in sight. Of course, that didn't mean he hadn't brought them. They could be hiding anywhere in this chaos. Obviously, their breakup hadn't improved his untidiness. He'd stuffed his clothes into the drawers with such wanton unconcern that it looked as if there'd been an explosion.

When she found herself itching to pull everything out and neatly fold it, she shook her head firmly. She was no longer his wife, and if he wanted to look as if he'd slept in his clothes, that was up to him. No one was going to point a finger at her and say she wasn't taking proper care of him.

That was another thing that had been wrong with their relationship, she suddenly realized. She'd spent too much time taking care of him instead of teaching him how to take care of himself. And she would have had to teach him. His mother hadn't cared if he had clean clothes, let alone how he took care of them. Indeed, he'd been lucky if she'd stayed sober long enough to remember to bring home food.

Annie supposed that's why she herself had been so tolerant of his bad habits and had jumped at his every whim. He'd had such a miserable childhood that she had wanted to make up for it. Since she'd been only eighteen when she married him, she hadn't had enough life experience to realize that by spoiling him she was only exacerbating his problems.

"Well, if by some horrible quirk of fate I do end up stuck with you again, some things are definitely going to change," she vowed when she finally found his underwear crammed in the bottom drawer behind another stash of jeans and T-shirts. As she crouched down to pull out what she needed, she continued, "You're not only going to learn how to fold your clothes and put them away neatly, you're going to learn how to do the laundry. I might even make you learn how to cook."

"You might make who learn how to cook?"

Tanner's question was so unexpected that Annie let out a yelp and almost tumbled backward to the floor. Still crouched, she swiveled toward the doorway, stating, "Dammit, Tanner! I told you not to sneak up on me!"

As her eyes found him, she gulped. He was wearing his robe, but it was so casually draped around his body that he might as well have been naked. Nearly the entire expanse of his muscular, hair-covered chest was exposed. Automatically, her eyes dropped to the narrow swatch of hair that trailed down his flat belly. It stopped at his belt, which was tied so loosely that it hung low on his hips and barely held the fabric together in the front.

A hot and wild yearning sprang to life inside her as she imagined walking to him, jerking off his belt and letting the fabric fall open. And then she'd touch him, cup him, stroke him, until he was hard and hot and quivering in her hand. And then . . .

She jerked her head up, bringing her imagination to a screeching halt. She may have agreed to give Tanner another chance, but she wasn't ready to go to bed with him. Sex had never been one of their problems—at least not in the traditional sense. It had been a problem in that Tanner had often dragged her to bed in the middle of an argument and made her so mindless with passion she couldn't even remember what they'd been arguing about. Only now did she realize that by doing that he'd invariably gotten what he wanted.

She narrowed her eyes as she regarded him. His expression was so innocent he could have passed for a choirboy, and that made her suspicious. He claimed that he wanted her back, and she suspected that he figured he could seduce her into capitulating. Did he really think she was that weak? That *stupid*?

"What are you doing up here, Tanner? I told you to wait downstairs."

He propped a shoulder against the doorjamb and drawled, "Well, Annie, this may come as a big surprise to you, but I don't have to do a blasted thing you tell me to do."

Annie started to issue a retort, but realized he was merely repeating the declaration she'd made to him down on the road.

"That's true," she said, a reluctant grin tugging at her lips as she stood. "But considering that one of the worst things you can do to an injured knee is go up and down stairs, your common sense should have told you I was right.

"Here are your clothes," she continued, tossing them to the bed. "Since you're here, you might as well get dressed. I'll see you downstairs."

"But what about my knee?" he asked, placing a hand on the other side of the doorjamb so that his arm blocked her exit.

"What about it?" she countered, cursing inwardly when she couldn't keep her gaze from dropping to his chest. With his arm upraised, his robe had parted even farther, and she saw one dark nipple peeking out from a whorl of silken chest hair. Again her imagination went rampant, and her pulse began to pound as she imagined caressing the nipple, feeling it grow hard beneath her fingertips. Then she'd touch it with her tongue and—

"You have to wrap it for me, remember?"

"What?" she murmured, blinking at him.

"My knee. You have to wrap it. Of course, if for some reason you'd rather I did it myself . . ."

The way his voice trailed off told Annie that he knew exactly what kind of effect he was having on her. She also recognized that he was daring her to get close to him, to touch him. She'd been right. The dirty rat was trying to seduce her!

Well, she could play the game as well as he could. If he wanted seduction, she'd give it to him. By the time she was done, he'd be so aroused that he'd have to spend the rest of the day out in the freezing rain just to be able to limp across the room!

11

"DID YOU BRING the elastic bandage with you?" Annie asked, a sexy note in her voice.

"It's right here," Tanner answered, barely holding back a cocky grin as he dropped his hand from the doorjamb and slipped it into the pocket of his robe. He'd obviously gotten her motor revved. Now all he had to do was get it racing. With the plan he'd cooked up in the shower, that should be a cinch.

When he pulled the bandage from his pocket, he faked a groan. As usual, Annie instantly took the bait. "What's wrong? Is it your knee?"

"No, it's not my knee, and it's nothing for you to worry about," he declared in his best I'm-in-horrible-pain-but-I'll-probably-live voice. "Here's the bandage."

Snatching it out of his hand, she grumbled, "If you say it's nothing for me to worry about, I need to worry. So tell me what's wrong, Tanner, and don't fool around," she warned. "I'm not in the mood to play games with you."

"Well, it's my back," he confessed. "I must have pulled a muscle when I fell on the road. It goes into spasms every now and then, but I'm sure I'll be all right."

She let out an exasperated sigh. "I can't believe this. First your knee and now your back. Go sit on the bed.

I'm sure there's some cream in the bathroom for muscle strain. After I've wrapped your knee, I'll rub it on your back."

Before he could respond, she tossed the bandage over her shoulder and headed for the bathroom. She was barely out of sight before he lost the battle with his grin.

"Yes!" he whispered, giving the air a victory punch with his fist and then wincing at the action. He hadn't been lying about his back. He had pulled a muscle, which was what had given him this idea in the first place. It just wasn't as bad as he was pretending. A good back rub should solve the problem, and there was nothing like a massage to get the hormones hopping.

Limping to the bed, he sat down on the edge and artfully arranged his robe so that all the essentials were covered—just enough so that while Annie wrapped his knee, she would be wondering if one wrong move would result in exposure. With any luck, the massage would push her over the edge and they'd end up in bed. He was sure that once they made love, everything would be okay.

But what if you aren't as good as Hank?

The thought came out of nowhere and startled the hell out of him. That she and this Hank guy might be lovers made him clench the bed covers in his hands. But even as jealousy threatened to overwhelm him, he forced himself to relax. He didn't like—hell, couldn't *stand*—the thought that she'd been with another man, but if she had been, he'd have to accept it. He'd just make sure their lovemaking was so spectacular that he wiped every trace of Hank out of her mind.

Even as he made that decision, he experienced a surge of doubt about his sexual prowess. He'd always believed that he and Annie had a fabulous sex life, but the truth was they'd both been virgins when they'd met. Since he couldn't remember his one disastrous encounter during his drunken night, he really had nothing with which to compare their lovemaking. Unfortunately, there was a good possibility that Annie did have a comparison, and that worried him. Was he as good as he thought he was? Could he compete with another man's lovemaking skills?

You're trying to stir up problems where there are none, Chapel.

God, he wanted to believe that. . . .

"I CAN'T BELIEVE THIS," Annie muttered in disgust as she dug through the top drawer of the bathroom cabinet. "Here I am all set to teach him a lesson, and he has a back injury. Why couldn't he have just fallen on his head? He couldn't hurt it if he tried."

She finally found the tube of analgesic cream and pulled it out. As she read the label, she discovered it was odorless. She would have preferred something that smelled to high heaven. Maybe if he had to live with the stink, he'd develop some sense. What kind of a fool went running after a skidding car, anyway?

An arrogant one, she concluded, and she knew that when it came to Tanner, arrogance was spelled with a capital *A*. He was so puffed up with his macho self-importance that she was surprised he didn't burst from it. Of course, she had to allow that he couldn't be any other way and do what he had to do. As the wife of another musician had once told her, there was nothing more arrogant than a man with a guitar. If he wasn't that way, then he'd never be able to climb up on a stage and put on a performance that would be so captivating people would be willing to pay to see him.

"Even if he does have to be that way, he's still a pain in the neck," Annie griped as she headed back to the bedroom.

She was so busy grumbling to herself that she'd almost made it to the bed before she took a good look at Tanner. The moment she did, she came to a stop so fast she nearly stumbled over her own feet. If his robe had been revealing before, it was now positively scandalous!

His shoulders were scarcely covered, and his entire chest was bared. His belt was still tied, but the fabric had parted at the waist, exposing his belly button and a tantalizing few inches below it. He'd tucked the robe between his legs, but she was sure that if he shifted even a millimeter, he'd be flashing her!

"Is something wrong, Annie?" he asked.

"No," she answered, her voice sounding unusually high-pitched. She frantically glanced toward his clothes, hoping that he'd put on his underwear. He hadn't. She considered telling him to do so, but realized that if she did, he'd know he had her rattled. That would be too dangerous a weapon to give him.

She had to clear her throat to say, "I, um, was, uh, just thinking. How's your back?"

"About the same."

"Oh, that's too bad. And your knee?"

He bent forward slightly to look at it. "It looks pretty swollen, don't you think?"

"Maybe a little," she answered, her voice again high-pitched. When he'd leaned forward, he'd dropped an arm between his legs. Her gaze wasn't focused on his knee, but on the fabric stretched tightly across the juncture of his thighs and outlining his very male attributes. And, yes, he did look a little swollen—tantalizingly so.

"A little?" he repeated, raising his head to frown at her. "It's at least twice the size of my other knee. I think that's more than a *little*."

"Um, well, yes, I suppose it is," she mumbled, dragging her gaze to his knee. "I'd better get it wrapped."

But even as she made the statement, she didn't know if she could do it. Just the thought of getting close to him had her stomach jumping and her pulse fluttering wildly. *Dammit!* she was supposed to be teasing him, not the other way around.

"Annie, is that good for the tube?" he suddenly asked.

"What?" she said, frowning in confusion.

He nodded toward her hands. "Is that good for the tube?"

She glanced down and realized that she was squeezing the tube of analgesic cream so hard that it was bulging at the sides. She immediately reduced the pressure, stating, "I'm, um, just making sure it's mixed well so it will work better."

"Oh," he said. "I didn't know you had to do that."

"Yes, well, it's a little-known secret," she muttered. "Shall we get your knee wrapped?"

"I'm ready whenever you are."

At his words, Annie had to close her eyes. Though she told herself he hadn't meant them *that* way, that didn't keep a tingle of excitement from zinging through her body.

Stop it! she ordered. *You aren't going to go to bed with him. It's too early for that!*

She opened her eyes, convinced she had enough willpower to resist him. With that resolve, she walked to him, tossed the tube to the bed and tugged the bandage off her shoulder. Kneeling in front of him, she looked at his knee. He was right. It was swollen to at least twice its normal size. She wasn't surprised. The way he'd been running around on it, he was lucky it wasn't worse.

She considered lecturing him, but changed her mind. He knew the right thing to do, and it was up to him to do it. Besides, it would take too much time to admonish him. Kneeling like this, she found her line of vision limited to the lower half of his body. The quicker she got his knee wrapped, the faster she could get away from that enticing view.

Training her gaze on his knee, she cupped her hand around his calf, urging his leg forward. As he moved it, his robe slid seductively up his thigh. She found herself hoping urgently for a quick peek underneath, and she had to close her eyes to make sure they behaved.

She was so focused on trying to gain control that she jumped and let out a startled gasp when his foot suddenly slid between her knees. Her eyes flew open, and she stared down at his foot, which was long and narrow and perfectly formed. She knew it was crazy, but desire suddenly burst to life inside her with an intensity she'd never experienced before.

Again her imagination ran rampant, and she envisioned what it would be like if she let her legs slide apart and drew his foot up, where she could rub herself against it. Just the thought caused heat to shoot down her thighs and her stomach muscles to clench with excitement.

This is crazy! she wailed inwardly. *You never considered his foot sexy before, so why are you doing it now?*

Because she wanted to make love with him, she realized, raising her eyes to his face. As she took note of the way his freshly washed hair tumbled across his forehead, and then let her gaze travel along the chiseled line of his cleanly shaved jaw, she acknowledged she wanted him so badly that it was like a fever burning inside her. She suspected that unless she gave herself what she wanted, it would continue to burn, getting hotter and brighter until it consumed her.

"Annie, if you don't stop looking at me like that, I am not going to be able to behave like a gentleman," Tanner suddenly drawled huskily.

The threat shimmered through her, sharpening her passion, and she boldly responded, "Well, I've been thinking of being very unladylike myself. What do you say, Tanner? Would you be willing to lay back and let me have my way with you?"

Her question shocked him, and he blinked at her, sure he'd misunderstood her. In all the years they'd been married, he'd always been the aggressor in bed, yet he couldn't deny that he was intrigued with the idea of just lying back and letting her make love to him.

"Well, considering my injuries, I suppose that it would make sense if you took charge," he said, his voice suddenly hoarse.

"So you wouldn't mind?" she questioned throatily, placing a hand on his good knee and scraping her short nails against his inner thigh. Then she smoothed the pads of her fingers across the area in a teasing circle.

"No, I wouldn't mind," Tanner rasped, almost coming up off the bed as her touch instantly telegraphed a message of excitement to his groin. When he felt his penis begin to swell, he quickly folded his hands across his lap, cursing the idiosyncracies of being a man. He didn't mind being aroused in front of Annie, but there was something disconcerting about it happening when he was practically naked and she was fully clothed.

"Then I'd better get your knee wrapped so we can begin," she said, sitting back on her heels.

When she lifted his foot and placed it in her lap, it seemed like such an innocent action that Tanner didn't even think about it. Then she parted her legs slightly, causing his foot to rest intimately against her. When she leaned forward to wrap the bandage around his knee, her pelvis pressed into his foot and she began to move slowly against him. Tanner become so aroused he thought he might explode from the pressure.

When she finished with the bandage, he instinctively reached for her, but she quickly scrambled backward on her knees, shaking her head as she insisted, "This is my game, remember?"

"Annie—"

"Tanner, you agreed."

He sucked in a deep breath and let it out slowly. He wanted to argue with her, but she was right. He had agreed, and he would play the game by her rules if it killed him. Right now he suspected it might.

He raised his hands in surrender. "I'm all yours."

"Good," she murmured, again sitting back on her heels before ordering, "Stand up and take off your robe."

He stared at her for a long moment, again acknowledging that it was disconcerting to reveal himself to her when she was fully clothed. It made him feel strangely vulnerable, and he didn't just mean physically. It gave him an odd sense of emotional defenselessness, as if he was exposing not just his body to her, but his soul, as well.

As he continued to stare at her, an ephemeral emotion flickered across her face. At first he couldn't put a name to it, but then he looked deeply into her eyes. They were clouded with the dreaminess of passion, but beneath the surface he perceived her own nervous vulnerability. He wasn't sure why she was nervous, but he knew he had to reassure her. And the only way to do that was to play her game.

Annie's heart lurched as Tanner slowly stood and undid his belt. When he finally pulled it apart and his robe fell open, she couldn't stop her gasp of awe. He was fully aroused and so beautiful that she could only stare in wonder. He shrugged out of the robe, and when it fell to his feet, her gaze moved over him with slow deliberation, taking in each muscled plane and hollow.

She'd always been awed by his physical beauty. Indeed, there were times during their marriage when she'd simply sat and stared at him, amazed that he was so perfect. Now she realized that when she'd lost him, all the beauty had gone out of her life. But she had it back, and even if it lasted no more than a few days or a few weeks, she was going to take full advantage of it.

She rose slowly to her feet and walked to him. He shivered when she stopped directly in front of him and trailed her hand from his shoulder to his hip in a butterfly caress.

"Are you cold?" she whispered, leaning forward to press a kiss against his chest, then flick her tongue against one of his dark nipples.

"No," he mumbled in a hoarse croak.

"Good, because I like seeing you this way," she murmured as she switched her attention to his other nipple.

When she continued to tease him, he gasped, "Annie, I can't take much more of this."

She laughed softly as she raised her head and looked up at him. "Then I guess I'll have to help you relax. Why don't you lay down on the bed and I'll rub the cream on your back."

He furrowed his brow and grimly stated, "Somehow I don't think a back rub is going to make me relax."

"Mmm, well, you'll never know unless you try it."

"There's only one thing I want to try right now." Suddenly he grasped her chin in his hand. Before she realized what was happening, his mouth swooped down to hers.

Annie started to protest, but he took advantage of her parted lips to slide his tongue into her mouth. She placed her hands against his chest to push him away, but she found her arms creeping around his neck instead. With a groan, he released his hold on her chin, wrapped his arms around her and crushed her against him.

Even through her clothes she could feel the scorching heat emanating from his body, and she shivered at the thrilling hardness of his erection when he cupped her bottom in his hands and lifted her so she was pressed intimately against him. As he lightly stroked himself against her denims, he began to tremble, and the tensing of his muscles told her he was fighting for control. Yet his kiss wasn't urgent. It was a long, slow and deep exploration that made her knees so weak she had to cling to him to remain standing. When he finally let her come up for air, she dropped her head to his chest and gasped for breath.

He rested his cheek against the top of her head as he said roughly, "Honey, if I'm not inside you in about two seconds, I think I'm going to die."

Annie wouldn't have believed that anything could make her any weaker than his kiss had. However, the image his words evoked was so erotic it made her sag in his arms as she breathlessly said, "Then I suppose you'd better get inside me."

Tanner didn't need any further encouragement. He quickly grabbed the bottom of her sweater and jerked it upward, and she lifted her arms so that he could pull it off. Then he reached for the front clasp of her lacy white bra.

He hadn't been kidding when he'd told her that he was about ready to die from his need to be inside her, but even the pulsing ache in his groin couldn't stop him from fondling her breasts as he pushed the fabric aside. Her roseate nipples were already hard peaks that spoke of her own arousal, and he couldn't resist them. As he pulled the bra straps down her arms, he lowered his head and drew one taut nipple into his mouth. Annie's gasp at the action caused repercussions in his groin that nearly made him come.

Realizing that his control was waning fast, he rose and lifted her in his arms. The muscle in his back contracted painfully and his knee protested at his hasty movement, but his overwhelming need to be inside her overshadowed any other pain.

Even as he lowered her to the mattress, she was kicking off her shoes and then reaching for the zipper on her pants.

"No, let me," he mumbled, his hands trembling as he pushed hers aside. "I need to see you. To touch you."

Annie couldn't breathe as she watched him undo her zipper. But instead of pushing off her jeans, he reached down to take off her socks. After he removed them, he knelt on the bed at her feet and lifted her bare foot. When he pressed the bottom of it to his erect penis and stroked himself against it, lust hit her with such force that her hips automatically arched upward. He dropped her foot and grasped the waistband of her jeans. Before her hips returned to the mattress, he had stripped her bare.

"Lord, you're beautiful," he rasped as he parted her legs and ran his hands up her inner thighs, making her arch again.

When she did, he caught her hips in his hands and lowered his head, treating her to an intimate kiss that propelled her toward climax.

But as she reached the crest, he raised his head, saying, "Not yet, honey. We're going to do this together."

As he spoke, he moved so that he was kneeling between her legs. When he came down over her, she wrapped her arms around his neck and her legs around his hips. The tip of his penis brushed against her in a maddeningly provocative way, and she gasped, "I need you inside me, Tanner!"

"Do you?" he murmured, nuzzling her ear as he rubbed himself against her teasingly.

He touched her most sensitive spot, and she again went spiraling toward climax. Just as she reached the peak, he flexed his hips and entered her. As her world exploded into ecstacy, he began to move urgently inside her. When she cried out her satisfaction, he increased his pace. She was still trembling when he reached his own fulfillment.

He collapsed against her and then rolled so that she was lying on top of him. They were still intimately joined, and she tightened her muscles around him, needing the reassurance that he was still a part of her. It was as if he, too, needed the reassurance, because he brought his good knee up so that her legs straddled his hips and her pelvis settled more deeply into his.

As he began to stroke her back from shoulder to hip, Annie buried her face in the hollow of his neck. She knew she needed to think about what had just happened between them, but for now she was content to lie here and let herself just enjoy him.

Tanner reveled at the feel of Annie's body cloaking him in hot, wet velvet, and he felt awed by the profundity of their lovemaking. True, it had been fast and wild, and he would have preferred to take more time. However, he didn't think that all the time in the world could have made their coming together better. Indeed, he doubted they'd ever be able to recreate that flash point of driving, mindless need, though he sure as hell looked forward to trying.

Just the thought made his body stir inside her, and he smiled wryly. If they stayed like this much longer, he'd be ready for another tussle, and he knew they had to talk before they made love again. As silly as it sounded, he needed to hear Annie's affirmation that their lovemaking had been as good as he believed. He also needed to hear her confirm that they were, for all practical purposes, again man and wife.

He took a deep breath and let it out slowly before asking, "Was it good for you, Annie?"

ANNIE HAD KNOWN that the blissful silence she and Tanner were sharing couldn't last forever, but she couldn't believe he would shatter it with such a ridiculous question.

Since she knew he couldn't possibly be serious, she joked, "Well, I don't know if it was good for me, but it was sure a heck of a lot of fun."

"Fun?" he gasped, rolling so suddenly that Annie found herself lying on her back with him looming over her, a scowl on his face. "That's all you have to say? That it was *fun!*"

"Well, what would you call it?"

"Well, I sure as hell wouldn't call it *fun!*" he roared.

Annie eyed him in confusion. She started to ask why he was so angry, but before she could, he said sneeringly, "Is that what you tell *Hank?* That it was *fun?*"

Though Annie knew it was the wrong thing to do, she couldn't help herself. She burst into uproarious laughter.

"There's nothing funny about this!" Tanner snapped.

"Oh, yes there is!" she said with a howl. "Oh, God, if Hank only knew!"

Propping a hand on either side of her head, he glared down at her. "Well, Hank is going to know, because you're going to call him and tell him that you're through."

He expected her to explode at that pronouncement, and he couldn't believe it when it only made her laugh harder.

She was hugging her sides and tears of hilarity were brimming in her eyes as she gasped, "I . . . can't do . . . that. Hank is—is . . ."

"Is what?" Tanner demanded impatiently.

"A woman!" she declared, bursting into fresh laughter.

Tanner was so stunned that he could only stare at her. When she finally started to regain control of herself, he said, "What do you mean, Hank's a woman? Yesterday you said he was a man."

She wiped her hands over her damp eyes. "No, you assumed she was a man. I just didn't bother to correct you."

"Why the hell not? Were you trying to make a fool out of me?"

Annie raised a brow at his accusing tone. Though she was tempted to tell him he managed to do that quite well on his own, she decided it would be a cheap shot. She had led him on, and in his place, she'd probably be mad, too.

"No, I wasn't trying to make a fool out of you, Tanner. I was just trying to keep some distance between us. If you'll recall, you'd been coming on to me. I figured that if you thought there was a man in my life, you'd leave me alone."

He frowned at her. "Well obviously, you were wrong."

"I guess I was," she admitted with a wry smile.

He smiled smugly in turn as he asked, "So when do you want to get married?"

Annie blinked. "I'm not going to marry you."

His mouth dropped open, and a moment later he yelled, "Annie, we just slept together!"

She let out an impatient sigh. "Tanner, just because I had sex with you doesn't mean I want to marry you."

"But of course you want to marry me," he argued. "You love me, and you can't deny that, because you told me so yourself."

"You're right," she allowed. "I do love you, but that doesn't mean I'm going to marry you."

"That's the most ridiculous thing I ever heard," he stated.

"Well, that's the way life is sometimes." She placed a hand against his chest and pushed until he reluctantly leaned away from her. When he did, she climbed out of bed.

"Where are you going? We're not finished talking."

"You might not be finished, but I am," she replied as she picked her clothes up off the floor. "I suggest that you get up and get dressed. We have work to do, and I'd like to get started right away."

"The work can wait. We need to talk about this," he insisted.

"I'm finished talking for now, Tanner," she stated firmly as she grabbed the last of her clothes. "I'm going to get to work. You can either join me or you can stay up here and sulk. The choice is yours."

When he didn't answer, she cradled her clothes against her chest and turned to face him. Lying there in his glorious nakedness with his blue eyes crackling with frustration, he reminded her of a fierce, golden god.

But he wasn't a god. He was a man, and she loved him so deeply and completely that it made her ache inside. For a moment—one brief, heart-wrenching moment—she wondered if she was making the right decision. He wanted her back, and she wanted to be with him. Would it be so wrong to just say yes and worry about their problems later?

Yes, it would be wrong. Until Tanner knew exactly what he felt and what he wanted, she'd be living in fear of losing him. The stress alone would probably ruin their chances of making it. If she ever went back to him, it had to be with the knowledge that this time it would be forever.

When he didn't say anything, but just continued to glare at her, she released an inward sigh and headed for the bathroom.

She'd just reached the doorway when he drawled, "I think there's something you need to consider before you so blithely turn down my marriage proposal. I didn't use protection when we made love, so it's possible that right this very second you might be getting pregnant."

His statement shocked Annie so badly that the room began to spin, and then everything went black.

12

"ANNIE!" Tanner yelled frantically as he watched her topple to the floor.

He bounded out of bed, but his knee gave out. Grabbing the edge of the mattress to steady himself, he cursed his body for failing him at a time like this. The moment he had his balance, he hurried to her, breathing a prayer of thanks that she'd fallen backward and landed on the thick carpeting rather than the hard tiles of the bathroom floor. Not that that didn't mean she hadn't hurt herself, he thought, terror shooting through him.

"Oh, dear God, Annie!" he declared hoarsely as he knelt beside her and discovered she was unconscious. Her face was white and her breathing shallow. He wanted to snatch her up in his arms, but even as he reached for her, he knew he couldn't do that. She might have some injury that he'd make worse by moving her.

He patted her cheek as he said, "Come on, Annie. Wake up. Please, honey, wake up. You have to wake up!"

His urgency must have reached her, because her lashes fluttered. Encouraged, he continued to pat her cheek. "That's it, honey. You have to wake up for me so I can find out if you're okay. Please, honey. Just open your eyes."

As if on cue, her eyes opened. "Tanner?"

"Yes, honey, it's me." Relief flowed through him. "Everything's okay. You fell, so you need to lie still until we figure out if you're okay. Do you feel any pain? I need to know if you're hurt, honey."

Annie's brain was so foggy that it took her a moment to get in touch with her body. When she did, she realized there were a few aches and pains, but nothing cried out that she was seriously injured. What had happened? All she could remember was making love with Tanner, and then . . .

Suddenly, memory came flooding back. She was glad she was still lying down, because she felt as if she might faint again. *Heaven help her, she might be pregnant!*

Two emotions assailed her at once—a mind-boggling elation and a soul-crushing terror. Having a baby was still her most cherished dream, but she'd already had one miscarriage. What if it happened again?

Even as her feelings began to war, the voice of reason surfaced. *Maybe it's the wrong time of the month.*

Clutching at that hope, she started frantically calculating. Within seconds she realized she was in a borderline situation. How could she have been so stupid?

With a miserable groan, she pressed her hands over her face.

"Annie, what is it?" Tanner demanded. "Do I need to call an ambulance?"

"No, you don't need to call an ambulance," she mumbled from behind her hands. "I'm fine."

"You are *not* fine," he stated grimly. "People who are fine do not pass out for practically no reason."

Annie lifted her hands from her face and stared at him incredulously. He couldn't really be so dense that he didn't realize how profoundly his words would affect her! But she knew he *was* that dense. She also knew she shouldn't be surprised. For her, pregnancy was a big deal. For him it was a "stupid mistake."

As the full impact of that hit her, she inwardly gasped, *Oh, my God, what have I done?* Unfortunately, she knew what she'd done. By going to bed with him, she'd made a grave error. How could she have let this happen? How?

She recognized that at this point, how wasn't the issue. It was what she did about it that mattered, and she knew there was only one thing she could do. She had to get away from Tanner, and she meant *away*, like in disappearing off the face of the earth.

She bolted to a sitting position and then scrambled to her feet. She'd just bent to scoop her clothes off the floor when Tanner caught her arm and said, "Annie, what are you doing?"

"I'm getting dressed, so let me go," she ordered, trying to tug her arm free.

But he just tightened his grip. "Honey, you just had a pretty bad fall and you may be hurt. Let me put you to bed and—"

"No!" she interrupted, panic surging through her. She couldn't let him be nice to her, and she sure couldn't get near a bed with him. If she did, they'd probably end up making love again, because she was just too darned weak to fight him.

Jerking her arm away with enough force that she broke his hold, she said, "I never want you coming near me again. Do you hear me, Tanner? *Never!*"

Tanner raked a hand through his hair. He'd known she might be disturbed by his reminder that they hadn't used protection, but this was too much. "Annie, honey, you aren't making any sense," he said soothingly. "Why don't you just lie down and rest? I'm sure the fall has rattled you. I'll go downstairs and make you some tea, and when you've calmed down, you'll feel better."

"After what you just pulled, I'm never going to feel better!" she yelled. "How could you stoop so low, Tanner? I know that you're about as insensitive as a rock, but how could you do this to me? Don't you have any decency at all?"

He was starting to get a little irritated. She was making him sound like some kind of unfeeling lout, and though he was willing to allow that he was sometimes a bit blunt, he was *not* insensitive or indecent.

Or at least he wasn't indecent in the way she was implying, he corrected, as his gaze roamed down her naked body. With her russet hair in a wild tangle, her arms akimbo and her feet braced apart, she looked like a sexy, fiery siren. He was tempted to haul her back to bed and show her just how good a trait indecency could be.

But even as he felt his body stirring at the thought, he recognized that making love with her wasn't going to solve what was going on. Indeed, in the mood she was in, it would most likely make it worse.

So instead of acceding to his baser instincts, he rose to his feet, stating, "Look, Annie, I don't know why you're overreacting like this. But if I made you upset, I promise I won't do it again."

"You're damn right you won't do it again, because you are never *ever* going to make love to me again!" she declared as she again bent to retrieve her clothes from the floor. Standing up and hugging them to her chest, she added, "And I want you to know that if I am pregnant, you aren't going to come anywhere near the baby. If I have anything to say about it, it won't even know that you're its father!" When she finished speaking, she spun around and marched toward the bathroom.

Tanner stared after her, confused. He would have thought that after losing her baby, Annie would be thrilled with the possibility of having another one. And what was this business about her not letting him near it? It would be his baby, too!

"Now, you just wait one minute," he said firmly as she reached the bathroom doorway. "You can't cut me out of my kid's life."

She shot him a glare over her shoulder. "Well, we'll just see about that, won't we?"

With that, she slammed the bathroom door, and the loud click that followed told him she'd locked it. At the sound, his resolve increased tenfold. She couldn't lock him out of her life that easily.

He limped to the door and then knocked on it, calling, "Annie! Open this door. Open it right this minute."

"Go to hell!" she yelled back.

"I'm not kidding, Annie," he warned. "I am not finished with this argument, so you either open this door and let me have my say, or I swear I'll break it down."

"You wouldn't dare!"

Tanner didn't even bother answering. He took a step back, braced his legs and then slammed his shoulder against the door.

ANNIE HAD JUST FINISHED putting on her underwear and was reaching for her sweater when the bathroom door suddenly reverberated with a sound so loud it made her yelp. Then she gaped at it in disbelief. The fool really was trying to break down the door! Was he nuts? For pity's sake, it was solid oak! *He'd* break before it would.

When she heard him hit the door again, she gave a flabbergasted shake of her head, deciding that when God had been passing out brains, Tanner must have been taking a nap. She also realized she'd better open the door before he killed himself.

"Dammit, Tanner! Stop it! I'm opening the door!" she yelled, undoing the lock and jerking the door open. Evidently he hadn't heard her, or else he had already been in full battering mode, because he came flying into the room shoulder first. She barely managed to get out of the way, and a moment later he slammed into the far wall and nearly fell to the floor.

As she watched him regain his balance, she realized that this entire scene was so silly it bordered on the absurd. Here he was, stark naked and trying to break down the door like some barbarian. She couldn't help it. She started giggling.

"What the hell is so funny?" Tanner snapped, rubbing his shoulder.

Knowing he wouldn't get the joke, she smothered another giggle and said, "Nothing. How bad did you hurt yourself?"

"I'll live," he grumbled, rubbing his shoulder again.

"That bad, huh?"

He scowled at her. "I said I'll live."

She smiled. "I'm glad to hear that."

Tanner couldn't think of an appropriate response, so he didn't say anything. He was also annoyed to realize that he'd not only just made a fool of himself, but he couldn't even continue the argument, because she was standing there smiling at him. Trying to argue with her at this point would be as ludicrous as trying to break down the door.

Dragging a hand through his hair, he said, "Look, Annie, I'm sorry for behaving like a fool, but you're driving me crazy. All I want to do is love you, but the more I try to do that, the more you fight me. Why won't you just let me love you?"

Why won't you just let me love you? He'd delivered the question with such touching directness that it wrapped itself around her heart and squeezed. He was right. The more he tried to love her, the more she fought him. Why?

All the obvious answers were there. Because of his obsession with his dream of becoming a star, his priorities were screwed up. She also wasn't sure if he really loved her or if he was in love with her ability to be his emotional sounding board, which, of course, allowed her to write the lyrics to his songs and keep his dream alive. Then there was her fear that he couldn't love a child, not even their child.

But even though she recognized that all those reasons were valid and real, there was another, more insidious reason why she kept fighting him. It was, quite simply, her own insecurity. As she'd already determined, he was too dynamic to be stuck with a shy, ordinary woman like herself. Deep inside, she didn't believe she was good enough for him and hadn't believed it from the first day she'd met him.

That realization rocked her to the core, because it made her take a hard look at herself and her own motivations. For years she'd told herself that she had catered to Tanner both emotionally and physically because of his miserable childhood, but now she understood that that was only partially true. She'd done it primarily because she'd wanted him to need her, to be dependent upon her. Subconsciously, she'd persuaded herself that as long as he needed her to survive, he wouldn't leave her.

But then he'd finally become a star, and with each passing day he'd seemed to need her less. The only thing she'd had left to give him—the only thing that would have allowed her to hold on to him—was a baby. It had been her security blanket, but it had been painfully snatched away. When she lost her child, she knew she had nothing left that would keep him with her. So she'd done what any insecure woman would have done. She'd run from him, and she'd been running ever since.

She was so staggered by the revelation that she felt dizzy once again, and she reached out to grip the counter. As her hand curled around its cold, marble edge, she accepted that it was time for her to stop running and find out the truth. If, by some miracle, Tanner really did love her, then they'd find a way to make it work. If it turned out that he didn't love her, at least she'd finally know.

"Annie, honey, are you all right?" Tanner questioned in concern as he appeared at her side and rested a hand on her shoulder.

"I'm fine," she lied, glancing up at him. The truth was she'd never been more scared in her life, because as long as she'd kept running, there had always been a spark of hope for her to hold on to. Now there was a chance that she'd lose even that. "And you're right, Tanner. It's time I stop fighting you and give us a chance."

"Oh, thank God," he whispered hoarsely as he pulled her into his arms. "I promise you won't regret it, Annie."

As she rested her head against his chest, she closed her eyes and prayed that he was right.

TANNER FRETFULLY STRUMMED some chords on the guitar. Annie was feeding her blasted cat, and he was waiting for her to join him in the music room. After she'd finally agreed to give them a chance, he'd tried to take her to bed. He wanted to show how much her decision meant to him by holding her in his arms and making love with her. She, however, had insisted that they come downstairs and work. He felt as if she was giving him what he wanted with one hand, but denying him with the other, and that frustrated the hell out of him. However, outside of playing caveman and dragging her to bed—and instinct told him that would definitely be the wrong move—he hadn't had any choice but to do what she wanted.

"Why does she always have to be so damn complicated?" he grumbled. He began to play the song he'd written last night and realized that, in some ways, the music reminded him of her. A composite of extraordinary highs and debilitating lows. A series of questions without answers, and conversely, answers without questions. It was as mysteriously alluring as she was, and just as maddeningly elusive. It was, quite simply, Annie.

With a sigh, he closed his eyes and began to play the song again, hoping against hope that somewhere in it was the key to understanding her.

ANNIE HAD JUST PLACED Pooh's food bowl on the floor when she heard Tanner begin to play his guitar. The melody wasn't one she'd heard before, and she automatically stopped to listen. After a few strains, she was shaking her head in awe. The music on his tape was beautiful and powerful, but this transcended all of those melodies put together. It was like being on an emotional roller-coaster ride that was out of control. One minute the music was plunging her into the depths of despair, and then moments later it sent her soaring to incredible heights of joy. It was poignant and yearning, whimsical and loving.

By the time he finished playing it, she could barely stand. Never had she been so moved, so *pummeled,* by a piece of music. And that was just how she felt—as if she'd been struck repeatedly, but not in a negative way. Indeed, if the melody had the right lyrics, she was convinced that it would be a masterpiece.

But as much as the music affected her deeply, profoundly, what stunned her was that this was the first piece of music he'd written that she didn't understand. Granted, she didn't always know exactly what his music meant when she first heard it, but she usually had a vague notion of what he was trying to say. In this instance, there was nothing. Not even a glimmer of intuition. It was as if he was revealing some secret part of himself that he had never exposed before.

When he began to play the melody again, she headed for the music room, feeling as drawn to it as the Pied Piper's victims must have been drawn to his music. By the time she reached the doorway, he was halfway into the melody. She stopped, gripping the doorjamb as she watched him. His eyes were closed, and his expression changed with each variation of theme in the music. He'd scowl and then he'd smile. He'd sigh heavily and then he'd laugh softly. At one point, she'd have even sworn she saw the glitter of tears on his lashes, though she told herself that had to be her imagination.

When he finally played the last note, she again shook her head in awe, but it wasn't just the music she was reacting to this time. It was Tanner's reaction to it. She'd never seen him so absorbed by his music. Normally he handled a piece he'd created with an almost detached distance, as if getting too close to it was more than he could bear. And in some ways that was probably true, because a lot of his music was a release of emotional pain. Though the lyrics she wrote were adult, the melodies were often a reflection of a lonely little boy desperately in need of love.

And that's what the difference was with this melody, she realized with a start. This was not the music of a sad little boy; it was that of a complicated man.

As if to give veracity to that thought, Tanner suddenly opened his eyes and turned his head toward her. As their gazes locked, she felt sucked into their startling blue depths. Though she couldn't name them, she could feel the emotions swirling through him, and there wasn't anything juvenile about them. That both intrigued her and frightened her, because one of the things that had always kept them on fairly equal footing was that she did understand his emotions. What she was sensing now went far beyond her comprehension and left her feeling as if she were treading on quicksand.

He broke the silence. "Well, what did you think of it?"

She had to clear her throat to speak. "It's a wonderful melody. The best you've ever written."

He nodded. "I figure with this song on the album, it's a sure shot to number one on the charts."

As the significance of what he was saying sank in, Annie cautiously asked, "You want to include this in the new album?"

"Of course. I know we'll have to drop out one of the other songs, but we'll just save it for album number three. This one's too good to hold back. Don't you agree?"

"Well, you may not have time to get it completed, Tanner. You have less than six weeks before your recording date."

He shrugged dismissively. "If you've done as good a job on the other songs as the one you sang yesterday, we can complete them in a week or two. That leaves us four or five weeks to whip this one into shape."

Annie had known where the conversation was heading, and she wasn't sure how to respond. He was so excited about the melody, as well he should be. He was right; it was too good to hold back. But she didn't see any other choice.

"There's only one problem with that, Tanner. I can't write the lyrics to that song."

He blinked at her. "What do you mean, you can't write the lyrics? Oh, hey, I get it. You have to clear it with Roy, right? We'll call him right now and get the go-ahead."

She shook her head. "This has nothing to do with Roy, Tanner. When I said I can't write it, I meant I *can't* write it. It's a beautiful melody, but it doesn't stir up anything creative inside me. It isn't speaking to me."

He bolted upright in the chair. "What do you mean, it isn't speaking to you? It has to speak to you. Dammit it, Annie! This music *is* you!"

She frowned at him in confusion. "What are you talking about?"

"Listen to the melody," he said as he started to play.

Annie closed her eyes and did as he instructed. Suddenly, he stopped playing and announced, "See? You do feel the music. I can see it on your face."

She opened her eyes and nodded. "I feel the music, Tanner. It moves me like nothing ever has before, but it isn't speaking to me. There is no way I can write the words. You'll have to get someone else to do it."

"No one else can do it. It has to be you or it won't be right."

Annie understood his frustration. Indeed, she shared it. He was correct—with the right lyrics it would probably hit number one. Such a boost to her career would be incalculable.

"Look, Tanner, why don't you tell me about the music," she proposed, coming into the room and sitting in the chair across from him. "When did you write it? *Why* did you write it? Maybe if I know the background, it will start stirring up my creative juices."

Tanner knew that what she was suggesting was reasonable, but he also knew he couldn't do what she was asking. Less than an hour ago she'd been furious with him over the possibility that their lovemaking might have gotten her pregnant. How would she react when he explained that he'd written the melody after he'd heard about the miscarriage? That the music had arisen from the hatred he felt toward himself for hurting her so terribly and for causing her such a horrible loss?

Even he found it bizarre that out of such misery had come such beauty. He was afraid she'd take it as a slap in the face, a sign that he was as insensitive and indecent as she'd claimed he was. Their relationship was so fragile now, so damn precarious. He feared that if he told her the truth, she'd walk out on him, and he couldn't—*wouldn't*—let that happen. He needed her too badly to lose her over a stupid melody, even if it would probably guarantee his success. If he'd learned nothing else from their divorce, it was that Annie was more important to him than that dream could ever be.

So, with a resigned sigh, he said, "Forget about this song for now. We can worry about it when all the others are done."

Annie was startled by his words. He'd been so insistent, so why was he changing his mind? She wanted to ask, but as she searched his face, she again felt that complex swirling of emotions inside him that she couldn't define.

Suddenly she recalled him saying that the music was *her*. What had he meant by that? Unfortunately, she suspected that she knew exactly what he'd meant. The music wasn't *her*; it was a reflection of his feelings for her.

On the surface, that sounded wonderful, because the melody was so beautiful. But instead of pleasing her, the thought sent a chill down her spine. The music might be beautiful, but she'd watched the conflicting expressions cross his face as he'd played it. She'd also felt that almost schizophrenic flow of emotions in the music. It meant his feelings were in turmoil, and until he had the words, he wouldn't really know how he felt about her.

The only person who could write those words was Tanner himself.

13

SOFT HAIR TEASED at Tanner's nose. With a sleepy sigh, he stretched his arm out to draw Annie's delicious body up against his, but all he encountered was a small ball of fur. His eyes flew open, and he found himself nose-to-nose with Pooh.

"What the hell are you doing in my bed?" he snapped, shooting into a sitting position and glaring at the cat. "You're getting cat hair all over the sheets!"

Pooh gave him a look of cat hauteur, sat back on his haunches and raised a back leg into the air. As he began to groom himself in a ribald manner, Tanner decided there must be something wrong with the beast. In the past week he hadn't growled, hissed or sprang at him once. Maybe he should suggest to Annie that she take him to the vet.

And speaking of Annie, where was she? he wondered, glancing toward the clock and frowning at the early hour. They'd worked until midnight and then they'd made love. She shouldn't be up and about. She should be sound asleep.

A wave of uneasiness drifted through him. During the past couple of days, he'd felt a change in her, though he couldn't quite figure out what it was. She'd been warm and open and loving, but he'd sensed something beneath the surface, a kind of frenetic energy. He supposed it could be because she was working too hard.

Indeed, she'd become a slave driver. In seven days they'd completed five songs, and had only one to go.

Well, two, he corrected, tossing back the sheet. They also had to write the one he'd come to think of as Annie's song. She was still insisting that it didn't speak to her, but he wasn't worried. Once the other songs were out of the way, she wouldn't feel so pressured. Then she could relax, and he was sure her Muse would start working like mad.

Pulling on his jeans, he stretched and walked to the window. It seemed impossible that a mere week ago an ice storm had moved through here. Spring had sprung in just a matter of days. The rolling green hills were bathed in sunshine, and he even spotted a small field of wildflowers beginning to bloom along the creek meandering through the property.

He suddenly recalled that Annie adored wildflowers, and an idea began to take form. She had turned down his earlier marriage proposal, but then he hadn't really asked her to marry him. He'd just assumed she would. How could he have been so stupid? Women liked to be romanced when it came to things like marriage proposals. No wonder she'd said no!

But today he'd remedy that. He'd coax her into taking a walk with him. He'd lead her to the creek, pick her a bouquet of flowers and formally propose to her on bended knee. If all went well, she'd say yes. Once they got the songs done, they would still have a few weeks before he was scheduled to record the new album, and that would be plenty of time to get married and go on a honeymoon. Since they hadn't been able to afford a real honeymoon the first time around, he'd make sure this one was wildly romantic.

Excited about his plan, he went in search of her. She was curled up in a chair in the music room, making notes on her notepad while listening to the last melody on the tape. As he watched her, he gave a wry shake of his head. Her hair was tousled, and she was wearing a silky white robe over a matching lace-and-silk nightgown that clung provocatively to her body.

Leaning against the door frame, he said, "Don't you know that all work and no play makes for a very lonely bed? I missed you."

Annie raised her head, and when her gaze landed on Tanner, she felt as if the breath had been knocked out of her. How could anyone look so darned sexy just climbing out of bed? His mussed hair and unshaved jaw enhanced his sensuality. His chest and feet were bare, and though he'd zipped his jeans, he hadn't snapped the waistband. The exposed flesh the open snap revealed made it apparent that he hadn't bothered to put on underwear.

Automatically, her gaze moved lower, and her pulse begin to race. She wanted to go to him and strip those jeans right off. Then, when he was standing there naked, she'd . . . She wasn't sure exactly what she'd do, because her mind was filled with such a jumble of naughty possibilities.

But as much as she wanted to indulge herself, she knew she couldn't. During the past couple of days she'd begun to realize that the longer she stayed, the harder it was going to be to retreat. She'd spent a week letting herself love him, but tomorrow morning she had to leave him. She was afraid that if she didn't, he might persuade her to stay forever, and she couldn't afford to do that. He needed some time alone. He had to write the words to his song. God knew, she feared that when he did, it might turn out to be a song that said goodbye. But, for both their sakes, she had to take that chance. And if it did turn out that he still wanted her, she'd come back to him in a flash.

But how was she going to explain that to him? It was a worrisome question, because she knew he'd feel that she was trying to hurt him. How could she make him understand that this was the only way to save them both from being hurt?

Realizing he was waiting for her to speak, she decided to worry about it later. She did, after all, have until tomorrow.

Waving her notepad at him, she said, "I missed you, too, but I think I've finally got this last song fine-tuned to perfection. Come on in and sing it for me."

"You want me to sing before I've had my first cup of coffee?" he questioned with mock horror.

She chuckled. "I'll tell you what. You sit down and read the lyrics, and I'll go get you some coffee."

He cocked his head. "If you're going to resort to bribery, you could be a little more inventive. How about some pancakes with the coffee?"

"Coffee first. Song second. Pancakes third, but only if you like what I've written. Otherwise it's cereal, because we'll have to go back to work."

He rolled his eyes. "I bet in an earlier life you were one of those drummers on a slave ship. You know, the ones where the men were chained to oars and forced to row to the beat of a drum."

"Yeah, well, I bet you were the slave we had to keel-haul because you were always so lazy you were one beat behind," she teased as she tossed her notepad to the coffee table and rose. "Read those lyrics, Tanner."

"Yes, ma'am!" he said with a caricature of a salute that made her laugh.

As she walked by him, he caught her around the waist and swung her up against him. "Where's my morning kiss?"

"Gosh, you want pancakes and a kiss, too?"

"Oh, yeah," he murmured, dropping his mouth to hers.

Annie sighed in pleasure as their lips met. It wasn't a passionate kiss, but one of teasing familiarity that stirred the embers of desire but didn't make them flare. As he released her and gave her bottom a fond pat, urging her toward the door, she realized that this was the part of their life she'd missed the most—the easy camaraderie, the feeling that they were not only lovers but friends. She only hoped that proved to be true.

When she returned with the coffee, Tanner looked up at her and grinned. "Damn, you're good, Annie. I don't even have to sing it to know it's perfect."

"Oh, no," she objected. "I got the coffee, so you have to sing. Otherwise, no pancakes."

"You can't fool me. You just want to hear my sexy voice," he drawled as he reached for his guitar.

He was right, but she wasn't about to confirm it. "Just sing, Tanner."

Sitting in her chair, she curled her legs beneath her and leaned her head back so she could listen to him. When he started, she watched him with fascination. Though he wrote his music with detachment, once he had the lyrics, he came alive. His blue eyes glittered with an internal light that was almost incandescent.

Each word brought a new emotion to his face that made his audience feel what he was feeling, see what he was seeing. Even though he was sitting, his body moved with a fluid grace that allured and enticed. Once again, Annie found herself comparing him to a god, and behind a guitar that was exactly what he was—a heavenly presence that made a listener believe in dreams.

By the time he was done, she knew that leaving tomorrow was the right decision, because watching him like this made her want to believe in his dreams. The problem was that it wasn't his dreams that could hold them together. In order for their relationship to last, they had to have *their* dreams.

"OH, COME ON, ANNIE! It's a beautiful day, and a little walk in the sunshine and fresh air is just what you need to get your creative juices flowing," Tanner coaxed, taking her hand and urging her toward the front door.

"Tanner, we really need to sit down and talk," Annie said, holding back. Twice during breakfast he'd brought up "The Song," as she'd so ominously come to think of it. He was convinced she could write the words, and though she'd again disabused him of the idea, he was refusing to listen. She'd hoped to put off telling him about her leaving until tomorrow, but now realized she had to do it almost immediately. The longer she waited, the more difficult it would be to make him understand why she was going.

"Annie, please. Just a short walk," he cajoled.

She knew she should refuse, but he was so darned hard to resist when he was standing there smiling at her.

"Okay, but just for a little while," she relented. "We need to talk, Tanner. And I mean really sit down and talk."

"After the walk," he assured her, linking her arm with his and leading her out the door.

"How's your knee?" she asked as they stepped off the porch.

"Just about good as new. Hardly even a twinge."

"Well, be careful out here. You don't want to hurt it again."

"I'll be careful."

They fell into a companionable silence as they wandered into the woods. Annie forced herself to forget their problems and let herself enjoy the warmth of the sun, the wonderful fragrance of pine trees and the richness of the earth.

When they arrived at the small creek that ran through the property, Tanner said, "Wait here. I'll be right back."

Annie sat down on the bank and pulled her legs up to her chest. Resting her chin on her knees, she watched the water race by tumbling over the rocks, then leaving them behind. That's how she felt right now, she realized—like she'd been caught up in Tanner's race to reach his dream, then left behind. How could she make him see that the old race was over and the dream was his? That it was now time for him to build new dreams, even if they didn't include her? She had to find the answers and fast.

"Don't look so solemn, Annie. It's time to be happy and celebrate."

His voice pulled her away from her thoughts, and she raised her head to look at him. He was holding a small bouquet of wildflowers, and suddenly he dropped to one knee in front of her. When he did, her heart began to pound in horror, because she knew what he was going to do. Oh, God, why hadn't she talked to him before now? This was going to make what she had to say so much worse!

"Marry me, Annie," he said huskily.

He looked so hopeful that tears welled into her eyes as she shook her head and whispered, "I'm sorry, Tanner, but I can't marry you."

Tanner could only gape at her. He had to have misunderstood her. After the wonderful week they'd shared, she couldn't possibly be refusing him!

"What do you mean, you can't?" he asked. "You *have* to marry me."

"Why?" she parried.

"Why?" he repeated. "That's a ridiculous question, Annie."

"Answer it anyway."

Sensing that his response was crucial, he sat down in front of her and studied the flowers in his hand. Obviously she was expecting something profound from him, and he had no idea what it was. Glancing up at her, he said, "You have to marry me because you love me."

"As I told you before, just because I love you doesn't mean I'll marry you."

"Well, what if you're pregnant?" he asked impatiently. "If you are, then you have to marry me. I was born a bastard, Annie, and no child of mine is going to bear that stigma."

"Tanner, your son already does."

Tanner felt as if she'd just punched him in the gut. He stared at her, shaking his head, but he wasn't sure if he was trying to deny her words or the sense of panic that was beginning to build inside him. *Dear God, his son was a bastard! How could he, of all people, have done that to him?*

"He's different," he declared hoarsely, unwilling—or perhaps unable—to deal with that realization. Unfortunately, that didn't stop the word *bastard* from repeating itself over and over in his head.

"Why is he different?" Annie asked.

"Why do you keep asking me all these damn questions?" he snapped.

"Because they're questions that need answers," she said with a heavy sigh. "So, tell me, why is your son different?"

"Because he's not my son. He's *her* son," he replied, surging to his feet. He paced a few feet down the bank and stared out across the creek to the thick growth of pines and underbrush on the other side. Why was Annie doing this?

"He's her son only because you haven't made an effort to make him yours," she said from behind him. "Tanner, he's three and a half years old. In all that time, haven't you ever wondered about him? Haven't you ever wanted to see him? Aren't you just a little bit curious about him?"

"No."

"Why not?"

He turned to face her, his expression one of anger. "How the hell do I know? I just don't care."

"You don't care, or you don't *want* to care?" she returned.

"There's no difference."

"Yes, Tanner, there's a big difference, because one implies apathy and the other fear."

"Why would I be afraid of a kid? That's stupid."

"When you consider the way you grew up, it's not stupid at all," she replied. "As a child, you learned to distance yourself from your emotions. It was easier for you not to feel, because if you didn't feel, you couldn't be hurt by your mother. The problem is, you're still distanced, and I think that just the thought of your having to deal with that little boy terrifies you. Deep inside, you feel that if you let yourself get close to him, you might end up getting hurt. So if you ignore him, you don't have to take any emotional risk."

"I don't believe this," he muttered, rolling his eyes. "I ask you to marry me, and you're psychoanalyzing me over a kid that's not even yours. For God's sake, why do you care? You of all people should be happy I don't want to have anything to do with him. How would you feel if I dragged him into your life?"

Annie winced at the question, and he immediately pounced. "You wouldn't like it, would you?"

"I'm not sure how I'd feel," she replied honestly. "I'd like to say that I would welcome him with open arms, but I don't know if I could."

"Then why are we even discussing this?" he asked in exasperation.

"Because if I'm right and you are afraid, then I have to believe that you'd be the same way with our child, and I know I couldn't handle that."

Her confession finally made some sense of this insane conversation, and Tanner exhaled a sigh of relief. He walked back and knelt in front of her again. Taking her hand in his, he said, "Annie, you're being silly. I would feel differently about your baby, because it would make you happy."

"I'm sorry Tanner, but that's the wrong answer."

He stared at her in disbelief. "What do you mean, that's the wrong answer?"

"It means that you should feel differently about it because it would be *our* baby and would make *us* happy, not because it would be my baby and make me happy."

"Dammit, Annie! It's the same thing."

"No, Tanner, it isn't, and the worst part is this is all my fault," she said, tears again welling into her eyes.

He shook his head in confusion. "Annie, you're not making sense!"

"Yes, I am."

"Then, please, explain it to me so I can figure out what you're talking about."

"I'll try," she said, rising to her feet and pacing down the bank as he had done. With her back to him, she said, "As I said before, you learned to distance yourself as a child, and you coped by pouring all your emotions into your music. But those emotions are often painful, so you won't let yourself explore them, which is why you can't write lyrics to your songs. By my writing lyrics for you, I'm taking your feelings and rubbing off all the sharp, painful edges. When I give them back to you, you can handle them, because you know that they might hurt a little, but they aren't going to cut."

"You're making me sound like an emotional zombie, and that's not true," he objected, surging to his feet. "If it was, I wouldn't love you."

She turned to face him. "I'm not sure you do love me, Tanner. I think that what you may be in love with is my ability to make your feelings safe enough for you to deal with them."

"That's totally ridiculous. I know what I feel for you, and it *is* love," he declared adamantly.

She shook her head again, and Tanner could feel the overwhelming sorrow emanating from her. "That isn't what your new melody says, Tanner. You think I should be able to write the words because that song is me. I think the reason it doesn't speak to me is because it's a reflection of your feelings for me. I'd like to believe those feelings are love, but I've watched your face when you play it. You have very conflicting emotions, and until you can sort through them, I can't possibly marry you."

"This is crazy," he muttered. "How am I supposed to sort through these supposed conflicting emotions?"

"I think a good start would be to write the words to the song," she answered. "When you do, you'll resolve some of your feelings. You'll know how you feel about your son. You'll know how you feel about me. But best of all, you'll know how you feel about yourself."

He shook his head. "I can't write the words without you, and you know it."

"You can write them, Tanner. All you have to do is open up your heart and feel. Once you've done that, then come to me. I'll be anxious to hear what you have to say."

"What do you mean, 'come to you'?" he asked warily.

"I mean that I'm leaving," she replied. A tear rolled down her cheek and she wiped it away impatiently. "I was going to wait until morning, but I think it's best if I go now. I'd appreciate it if you'd stay away from the cabin until I'm gone. It won't take me very long to pack."

Before he could even assimilate her astonishing announcement, she gave him the saddest smile he'd ever seen and said, "I love you, Tanner. Goodbye."

He could only stare at her in disbelief. She loved him, but she was leaving him. It didn't make any sense! As she walked away from him, her shoulders sagging, he told himself to run after her. To grab onto her and refuse to let her go. She didn't know what she was talking about. He *did* love her! But by the time his brain managed to convince his body that it had to move, she had already disappeared.

"This isn't happening," he whispered hoarsely. "It can't happen. I don't know how to live without her. She has to stay with me or I'll die."

But it was happening, and as the realization sank in that she was really leaving, he fell to his knees, dropped his head back and screamed at the sky, "Annie! Please! Don't leave me!"

The only response was the terrifying echo of his own frantic voice.

"ANNIE, YOU HAVE TO EAT," Lisa scolded as Annie pushed her untouched dinner plate away. "Remember, you're probably eating for two now."

"Oh, God, don't remind me," she mumbled as she folded her arms on the table and rested her head on them. It had been over three weeks since she'd left Tanner, and she hadn't heard a word from him. Since she hadn't, she could only assume the worst. "How could I let this happen, Lisa? Why was I so stupid?"

"Love isn't stupid, Annie. It just hurts like hell sometimes," her sister said, consolingly.

"Tell me about it," She groaned, sitting up and protectively rubbing her stomach. Since she was nearly two weeks late, she was sure she was pregnant. She'd considered trying one of those home pregnancy tests to confirm it, but had chickened out at the last minute. She hadn't been much further along than this when she'd miscarried. She knew it sounded silly, but she felt that if she didn't know for sure, then nothing horrible could happen. And if she was pregnant, it would kill her to lose the baby. It looked as if it was going to be the only part of Tanner she'd have left.

Tears welled into her eyes at the thought, but she willed them away and pulled her plate back in front of her. If something bad did happen, it wasn't going to be because she hadn't taken proper care of herself. She was going to eat, and she was *not* going to let herself be depressed.

"I wish you'd come home with me so I could keep an eye on you," Lisa fretted. "I don't like you being here all by yourself when you're upset."

"I'm fine," Annie said, forcing a reassuring smile. Her sister had been trying to get her over to her house ever since she'd come home, but if Tanner did come looking for her, she had to be here. "Honest, I am. Besides, you have a husband and three kids to worry about. You don't need another person underfoot."

"Annie, you wouldn't be underfoot!"

"Well, I might not be, but Pooh would. He's being particularly obnoxious these days. If I didn't know better, I'd think he misses Tanner."

Lisa chuckled and shook her head. "Now that would be a miracle, Pooh and Tanner getting along. But I guess stranger things have happened."

"Not much stranger," Annie stated dryly.

"Well, I'd better get going," Lisa said, glancing at her watch. "Are you sure I can't talk you into coming home with me?"

"I'm sure. Stop worrying about me."

Lisa gave her a grim look. "You're my baby sister, Annie. I'm always going to worry about you."

"Well, do it from your own home. Now get out of here. You have a husband and children who need you."

"Okay, I'm gone." Rising and coming around the table, she gave Annie a hug. "Call if you need me."

"I will. Now go."

When Lisa finally left, Annie gave a sigh of relief. She loved her sister, but sometimes her mothering got on her nerves. After rinsing her dinner plate and putting it into the dishwasher, she went into the living room. She switched on the television, but after flipping through all the channels, couldn't find anything that caught her attention. She considered turning on the radio, but the last thing she was interested in right now was music. Finally, she did what she'd been doing repeatedly for the last three weeks. She leaned back against the sofa cushions, closed her eyes and relived the time she'd spent at the cabin with Tanner.

She was so deep into the memories that when she first heard the music, she thought it was in her mind. But then Pooh came running into the room with a yowl. Her eyes flew open and she watched him leap onto the sill to look out the open window. It was then that she realized the music was coming from outside, and her heart skipped a beat. Tanner was here, and he was playing his song. Oh, God! He was here! What did that mean?

With a gasp, she rose from the sofa and hurried to the second-story window. As she looked down, she saw Tanner's silhouette in the lights from the parking lot. When he caught sight of her, his hand dropped away from the guitar. They stood there, staring at each other, for what seemed an eternity. Though Annie knew she should do or say something, she couldn't move. Couldn't breathe. Couldn't think. All she could do was pray that this meant what she hoped it did, because if it meant goodbye, she'd die.

Then Tanner started playing the guitar again. After the first few strains, he sang,

"I was lost and hurt
The day that I met you
But then you took my hand
And I knew that dreams came true

From the first it was magic
But I knew it couldn't last
Then I found a secret
That kept you in my grasp

I gave you my music
You gave me your words
Together we wrote the kinds of songs
That soared with the birds

But loving dreams ain't easy
Hardest thing I've ever done
Because you are the perfect dream
To love and keep from harm

That meant I had to hurt you
So you'd see me for what I am
I'm not the god you view me as
I'm just a mortal man

Living now without you
I know that I was wrong
Without you I am nothing
As long as you are gone

I need you, need your music
Or I'm hurt and lost again
Together we'll build a legacy
That will never, ever, end

Oh, yes, I promise, darling
That if you come back to me
Our legacy of dreams
Will never, ever, end"

When he'd played the last note, he cried, "I love you, Annie O'Neill-Chapel! Do you hear me? I *love* you!"

"Oh, God, I love you, too," she whispered, too overcome with emotion to speak any louder.

When he yelled, "Can I come up?" she nodded and waved.

By the time she managed to get to the door, he was bursting out of the stairwell and running down the hall. She stepped out and opened her arms to him. When he reached her, he caught her around the waist and pulled her into a tight hug. Then he backed her into the apartment and shut the door. Leaning against it, he braced his legs apart and pulled her into the cradle of his thighs.

Framing her face in his hands, he said, "It's true, Annie. I love you so much I can't stand it. You're everything I want. You're everything I need. Nothing else matters, and I mean *nothing*."

"Not even your dream of stardom?" she asked tremulously.

"Especially not the dream," he answered, "because as I said in the song, you're my perfect dream."

"Oh, Tanner," she said, tears spilling down her cheeks. "I love you, too, and you've always been my perfect dream."

Once again he hugged her to him tightly. After several seconds passed, he caught her chin in his hand and tilted her head upward. "I want you to marry me, Annie, but before you give me an answer, there's something you should know. I've done a lot of thinking about my son. You were right when you said that I'd made a mistake, but he's the one who's been paying for it. I may not feel like it, but I am his father. That's why I can't desert him like my own father deserted me. I have to try to do the right thing by him. I don't know if it will work out, but it is possible he'll become a part of my life. If that happens, can you deal with it? Or will it be too hard for you?"

Annie closed her eyes at the questions. Would it be too hard for her? Could she accept the boy into her life? Even as she considered her feelings, her hand was creeping to her abdomen. What if she had another miscarriage? What if . . .

She stopped herself. The baby was her dream, but it was no longer a security blanket. No matter what happened, she knew she'd always have Tanner's love. She also knew she had to support him in this. Dealing with his son would be another step in learning how to shed his emotional baggage from the past. It was going to be a long process, and she didn't expect overnight miracles. But by finding the courage to face the boy, he would also be learning how to open his heart to their own child. He was finally on his way to becoming whole and finding peace.

Opening her eyes, she said, "I can deal with it. He's a part of you, Tanner, and that means he'll be a part of me."

He searched her face for a long moment, as though needing reassurance, and then nervously smiled. "Then I guess that leaves only one unsettled matter. Will you marry me?"

"Well, before I answer, I think there's something you should know," she hedged.

He regarded her warily. "What's that?"

"I'm pretty sure I'm pregnant."

"Oh, my God!" he stated hoarsely. "What are you doing standing up? Why aren't you lying down? Are you feeling all right? Oh, my God! I didn't hurt you when I hugged you, did I?"

Before Annie could respond, he gently lifted her in his arms and carried her to the sofa. Laying her down on it, he bent over her and said, "Is there anything I can do for you?"

"Well," Annie murmured as she linked her own arms around his neck. "The first thing you can do is let me say that yes, I will marry you. Then you can give me a kiss. After that, things are pretty much up for grabs."

"Ah, Annie," he murmured as he lowered his lips to hers. "I love you so much, and I promise that I'm going to devote my life to making you—no, *us*—happy."

Any doubts Annie may have had disappeared beneath his tender kiss. It said everything his song had said, and so much more.

INHOUSE MEMO
NCR RECORDS

DATE: January 2
TO: Roy Wilson, CEO, NCR
FROM: Publicity Department
Mr. Wilson: The following clipping is from today's newspaper gossip column, "Country Towne." Please advise on how we should respond to the last paragraph.

Country Towne
Superstar country-and-western singer, Tanner Chapel and his wife, lyricist Annie O'Neill-Chapel, seem to be on a roll. They ended last year with Chapel's current album number one on the charts, and both are expected to be nominated for several music awards.

Yesterday they started the New Year with a bang, when Mrs. Chapel gave birth to a daughter. At the time of this writing, no name for the newest member of the Chapel family had been selected, but hospital officials say that mother and daughter are doing fine. It seems, however, that Mr. Chapel had a minor accident upon returning home from the

hospital. No details have been released, but an inside source claims that the accident was caused by
someone named Pooh. (Spelling of this name has
not been verified.) "Country Towne" will keep you
posted on both the baby's name and the details of
Mr. Chapel's accident.

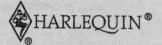

THE VENGEFUL GROOM
Sara Wood

Legend has it that those married in Eternity's chapel are destined for a lifetime of happiness. But happiness isn't what Giovanni wants from marriage—it's revenge!

Ten years ago, Tina's testimony sent Gio to prison—for a crime he didn't commit. *Now* he's back in Eternity and looking for a bride. *Now* Tina is about to learn just how ruthless and disturbingly sensual Gio's brand of vengeance can be.

THE VENGEFUL GROOM, available in October from Harlequin Presents, is the fifth book in Harlequin's new cross-line series, **WEDDINGS, INC.** Be sure to look for the sixth book, **EDGE OF ETERNITY,** by Jasmine Cresswell (Harlequin Intrigue #298), coming in November.

WED5

MILLION DOLLAR SWEEPSTAKES (III)

No purchase necessary. To enter the sweepstakes and receive the Free Books and Surprise Gift, follow the directions published and complete and mail your "Win A Fortune" Game Card. If not taking advantage of the book and gift offer or if the "Win A Fortune" Game Card is missing, you may enter by hand-printing your name and address on a 3" X 5" card and mailing it (limit: one entry per envelope) via First Class Mail to: Million Dollar Sweepstakes (III) "Win A Fortune" Game, P.O. Box 1867, Buffalo, NY 14269-1867, or Million Dollar Sweepstakes (III) "Win A Fortune" Game, P.O. Box 609, Fort Erie, Ontario L2A 5X3. When your entry is received, you will be assigned sweepstakes numbers. To be eligible entries must be received no later than March 31, 1996. No liability is assumed for printing errors or lost, late or misdirected entries. Odds of winning are determined by the number of eligible entries distributed and received.

Sweepstakes open to residents of the U.S. (except Puerto Rico), Canada, Europe and Taiwan who are 18 years of age or older. All applicable laws and regulations apply. Sweepstakes offer void wherever prohibited by law. Values of all prizes are in U.S. currency. This sweepstakes is presented by Torstar Corp, its subsidiaries and affiliates, in conjunction with book, merchandise and/or product offerings. For a copy of the official rules governing this sweepstakes offer, send a self-addressed, stamped envelope (WA residents need not affix return postage) to: MILLION DOLLAR SWEEPSTAKES (III) Rules, P.O. Box 4573, Blair, NE 68009, USA.

SWP-H994

HARLEQUIN® Temptation®

HART GIRLS

Bestselling Temptation author Elise Title is back with a funny, sexy trilogy—THE HART GIRLS—written in the vein of her popular miniseries THE FORTUNE BOYS!

Rachel, Julie and Kate Hart are three women of the nineties with heart and spark. They're determined to win the TV ratings wars—and win the men of their dreams!

Stay tuned for:

#509 DANGEROUS AT HEART (October 1994)
#513 HEARTSTRUCK (November 1994)
#517 HEART TO HEART (December 1994)

Available wherever Harlequin books are sold.

ETST

HARLEQUIN®

Temptation®

Lost Loves

RIGHT MAN...WRONG TIME

Remember that one man who turned your world upside down? Who made you experience all the ecstatic highs of passion and lows of loss and regret. What if you met him again?

If you missed any Lost Loves titles, here's your chance to order them:

Harlequin Temptation®—Lost Loves

#25589	THE RETURN OF CAINE O'HALLORAN by JoAnn Ross	$2.99	☐
#25593	WHAT MIGHT HAVE BEEN by Glenda Sanders	$2.99 U.S. $3.50 CAN.	☐ ☐
#25600	FORMS OF LOVE by Rita Clay Estrada	$2.99 U.S. $3.50 CAN.	☐ ☐
#25601	GOLD AND GLITTER by Gina Wilkins	$2.99 U.S. $3.50 CAN.	☐ ☐
#25605	EVEN COWBOYS GET THE BLUES by Carin Rafferty	$2.99 U.S. $3.50 CAN.	☐ ☐
	(limited quantities available on certain titles)		

TOTAL AMOUNT	$
POSTAGE & HANDLING	$
($1.00 for one book, 50¢ for each additional)	
APPLICABLE TAXES*	$_____
TOTAL PAYABLE	$_____
(check or money order—please do not send cash)	

To order, complete this form and send it, along with a check or money order for the total above, payable to Harlequin Books, to: **In the U.S.:** 3010 Walden Avenue, P.O. Box 9047, Buffalo, NY 14269-9047; **In Canada:** P.O. Box 613, Fort Erie, Ontario, L2A 5X3.

Name: _____

Address: _____ City: _____

State/Prov.: _____ Zip/Postal Code: _____

*New York residents remit applicable sales taxes.
  Canadian residents remit applicable GST and provincial taxes.

LOSTF

This September, discover the fun of falling in love with...

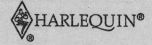

Harlequin is pleased to bring you this exciting new collection of three original short stories by bestselling authors!

**ELISE TITLE
BARBARA BRETTON
LASS SMALL**

LOVE AND LAUGHTER—sexy, romantic, fun stories guaranteed to tickle your funny bone and fuel your fantasies!

Available in September wherever
Harlequin books are sold.

HARLEQUIN®

HARLEQUIN®

Don't miss these Harlequin favorites by some of our most distinguished authors!
And now you can receive a discount by ordering two or more titles!

HT #25525	THE PERFECT HUSBAND by Kristine Rolofson	$2.99 ☐
HT #25554	LOVERS' SECRETS by Glenda Sanders	$2.99 ☐
HP #11577	THE STONE PRINCESS by Robyn Donald	$2.99 ☐
HP #11554	SECRET ADMIRER by Susan Napier	$2.99 ☐
HR #03277	THE LADY AND THE TOMCAT by Bethany Campbell	$2.99 ☐
HR #03283	FOREIGN AFFAIR by Eva Rutland	$2.99 ☐
HS #70529	KEEPING CHRISTMAS by Marisa Carroll	$3.39 ☐
HS #70578	THE LAST BUCCANEER by Lynn Erickson	$3.50 ☐
HI #22256	THRICE FAMILIAR by Caroline Burnes	$2.99 ☐
HI #22238	PRESUMED GUILTY by Tess Gerritsen	$2.99 ☐
HAR #16496	OH, YOU BEAUTIFUL DOLL by Judith Arnold	$3.50 ☐
HAR #16510	WED AGAIN by Elda Minger	$3.50 ☐
HH #28719	RACHEL by Lynda Trent	$3.99 ☐
HH #28795	PIECES OF SKY by Marianne Willman	$3.99 ☐

Harlequin Promotional Titles

#97122	LINGERING SHADOWS by Penny Jordan	$5.99 ☐
	(limited quantities available on certain titles)	

	AMOUNT	$
DEDUCT:	10% DISCOUNT FOR 2+ BOOKS	$
	POSTAGE & HANDLING	$
	($1.00 for one book, 50¢ for each additional)	
	APPLICABLE TAXES*	$_____
	TOTAL PAYABLE	$_____
	(check or money order—please do not send cash)	

To order, complete this form and send it, along with a check or money order for the total above, payable to Harlequin Books, to: **In the U.S.:** 3010 Walden Avenue, P.O. Box 9047, Buffalo, NY 14269-9047; **In Canada:** P.O. Box 613, Fort Erie, Ontario, L2A 5X3.

Name: _____

Address:_____City: _____

State/Prov.: _____ Zip/Postal Code: _____

*New York residents remit applicable sales taxes.
 Canadian residents remit applicable GST and provincial taxes..

HBACK-JS

30422869R00071

Made in the USA
Middletown, DE
23 March 2016

Presented to

By

Date

I LAUGH AT
THESE
SKINNY
GIRLS

POETRY FOR PEOPLE
WHO HATE POETRY II

heART of
WORDS
CO.UK

Also by Tolu' Akinyemi

Your Father Walks Like A Crab
(Poetry for People Who Hate Poetry)

///////////////////////////

Coming soon

To Cook A Stone
(Poetry)

Bobolaya The Land Of Liars
(Folktale)

This Bus Has Room For Forty People
(An illustrated and very cheesy little book for people in love)

I LAUGH AT THESE SKINNY GIRLS

POETRY FOR PEOPLE
WHO HATE POETRY II

TOLU AKINYEMI

I LAUGH AT THESE SKINNY GIRLS

Copyright © 2015 by Tolu Akinyemi. All rights
reserved. Printed and published in the United
Kingdom. No parts of this book may be used
or reproduced in any manner whatsoever
without written permission, except in the case
of reprints in the context of reviews.

All work herein by Tolu' Akinyemi

Heart of Words Publishing
is a trading name of
Strange Ideas UK Limited

www.heartofwords.com
www.strangeideas.co
www.poetolu.com
books@poetolu.com

First published May 2015

This imprint, September 2015

ISBN: 9789785359718

Cover design by Tolu Akinyemi

This book is a work of fiction. Except where
stated otherwise, names, characters, places
and incidents either are products of the
author's imagination or are used fictitiously.
Any resemblance to actual events or locales or
persons living or dead are unintentional.

For the one,
The One I'm
looking for

CONTENTS

Part 2

Part 3

PREFACE

I certainly cannot be the only one who has noticed how simple the word 'simple' sounds, unlike the word 'complicated' which simply sounds...complicated.

(I'll admit I have often wondered, perhaps time and familiarity subtly reshapes our perception, making us associate the 'look' of words on paper to their meanings in our minds, luring us into thinking they sound and look, like what the dictionary says they mean, but that is a matter for another time).

I love 'simple things' for their ability to be nonchalantly potent. A simple 'hello' can secure a lifelong friend, a simple apology can redeem a would-be enemy, a mere remark can cost a man his life and casual but careless words can cause two nations to war.

An understanding of the power of 'simplicity', tacitly taught me the efficacy of simple words and how they are the vehicles of useful communication. I learnt that often, 'less says more', I also realised how very silly it is to say simple things complicatedly.

How we often crave so direly
The depths of hefty words
To convey outwardly
Emotioning inner thoughts.

How we yearn the beauty
Of gargantuan rhetoric
To flush out entrapped feelings
To ears that need to hear it.

But I know better than try hard
To say simple things complicatedly
Like when "I'm really sorry"
Or telling you "I love you".

Few years ago, I really began to find poetry fascinating, but I also realised that a lot of people do not share my enthusiasm about poetry. It was more startling, discovering that many of such people are already avid readers, yet for them, poetry is strictly off the menu.

There appeared to be a very simple reason for this; a 'hatred' of poetry because they find it ostentatious and poets egoistic. They also consider poetry typically boring and obscure, especially when they struggle to understand or enjoy what is conventionally 'touted' as brilliant poetry.

Before I learnt 'the simple lesson', I stupidly believed the quality of poetry could be proportional to the time it takes readers to grasp its message. I judged its beauty by how well-entrenched the meanings were, but I have found that the duty and skillfulness of a poet is not in how well he hides beautiful meanings between the lines, it's in how easily he reveals them. A poem does not have to be difficult to be deep; 'simple' and 'deep' are not mutually exclusive.

Like every form of art, poetry is a means of communication and as such, its consumption does not have to be a puzzle-solving exercise. It should be like a walk in a beautiful garden, alive with exotic flowers and animals; a garden of words in which each turn presents delights that tickle the eyes.

I learnt that poetry is a language or a message, and the poet is a mere courier. Poetry is a means of communication and its glory is its successful delivery. The fanciful words and pedantry a message is encased in is worthless, if the message is undelivered, and if the message is undelivered, the messenger (poet) has failed, and if the messenger fails, the message is in vain.

This understanding made me start calling my poetry *'poetry for people who hate poetry',* which can be described as poetry marinated in; detail, simplicity, relatability, vividness and wittiness. So far the feedback has been encouraging. Many readers speak of how they now see poetry in a new light.

Without any intention to ridicule or undermine complex forms of poetry, the poems in this book are written without the strictures of conformity and with a form and motive to portray poetry as enjoyable, especially to those people who would normally consider poetry intimidating or boring.

I Laugh at These Skinny Girls is the second book in the *'poetry for people who hate poetry'* series and I really hope you enjoy reading these poems as much as I did writing them.

Tolu' Akinyemi

May 2015
Abbey Wood, London

Part One

276 GIRLS *

A fowl is missing from the next village.
That night they heard a shriek,
A snap, retreating feet and silence.
Jòná says "who cares?
It is not my fowl".

Then a goat was stolen six streets away
We found clean bones and spices
And remorseful cooking devices
But there was no goat.
Jòná says "who cares?
It is not my goat".

Then some girls were stolen
From across the street
While still suckling
On their mothers' teats
The men were in no hurry,
They waited for dinner
Stole the girls and the cutlery.
Jòná says "who cares?
It is not my cutlery".

* On the 14th of April 2014, in Chibok, a town in Northern Nigeria, West Africa, about 300 girls were abducted from their school, by a terrorist group called Boko Haram. Despite the massive international media attention the tragedy was exposed to, the girls are yet to be rescued (as at the time of going to press with this book).

The moon and stars are shy tonight
As hefty men leap over the fence.
We hear heavy footfalls outside the wall
Then a noise on the roof
Jòná whimpers, "Could that be my roof?"
Soon we hear a knock, a very loud one
On the centre of *Jòná's* door.

BRING BACK OUR GIRLS†

In the homes of
Two hundred and seventy-six
Helpless family heads
The tiny beds of
Two hundred and seventy-six
Stolen girls gather cobwebs.

No one slept
In them yesterday
And today
And forever?

† On the 14th of April 2014, in Chibok, a town in Northern Nigeria, West Africa, about 300 girls were abducted from their school, by a terrorist group called 'Boko Haram'. Despite the massive international media attention the tragedy was exposed to, the girls are yet to be rescued (as at the time of going to press with this book).

MOTHER SAID

Mother said, daughter
Never chase a man
But be at quarters
And let him
Come running
If he wants.

Mother said, daughter
If you chase a man
You will be behind
In his fart's line of fire
And know now daughter
Men's fart
Smells really bad.

THE BUS TO KADUNA

The road was dry
The sun was high
And on the bus to Kaduna
Adearla sat a row behind
A lady with a purple hat.

The hawkers came, the hawkers left
But not before they sold their wares
Of roasted corn and chippy fries
And nuts and buns and scrambled eggs.

Then after ten or thirteen miles
The lady in the purple hat
Began to shift from left to right
And slowly made to raise a thigh.

So from behind, *Adearla* had
To gently tap her shoulder pad
And calmly say "please don't do that"
"Don't do what?" The lady asked.

Adearla made a pleading sigh
And said "please!
Don't ease out that fart!"

HALIMA

Halima sits outside with Mama
Discussing signs of harmattan.

Mama says "my fine daughter
You are not getting younger
And soon (not later)
You should snatch for yourself
A rich handsome husband".

"You are right" replied *Halima*
Whose husband shall I snatch?

BLUR

Nostalgia will soak
Like a bread loaf in a wet bowl
As memories tumble
Downhill like rolling stones.

Don't you remember
When we were younger
And all that mattered
Was growing up faster?

Boys painted on beards
With stolen school chalk
Girls wore their mother's bra
Stuffed with colourful socks
Then we all grew up
In a quick blur.

It's a Monday morning and
Crazy grown-ups are in a hurry
Racing like rats
To places far from their hearts.

If you see me daydreaming
Don't call me lazy,

I only miss being young
And days I wondered why
Adults watched the boring news
Instead of funny cartoons
And food got on the table, how?
We never knew, (never had to).

All that mattered
Was growing up faster
And no one warned
We'd be stuck in a chore.

Now it's late
To relive a childhood
Gone in a haste
But who would hear it
That evening too
Caught me unprepared?
Distracted by routines
Chasing the wind
With dreams still un-lived
And a bucketful of lists.

WHICH ONE?

Mama asks
"This one?"
She responds
"No way!
He is short".

Mama asks
"This one?"
She responds
"No way!
The belly bulge".

Mama asks
"This one?"
She responds
"No way!
The starving purse".

Mama asks
"This one?"
She responds
"No way!
The balding spot".

Mama asks
"This one?"
She responds
"No way!
The facial pores".

Mama asks
"This one?"
She responds
"Yes! He's the one!"

Mama replies
In shock
"But he is short?"

SATURDAYS

"Do you know *Yéwandé*
Will get married on Saturday?"
'Reveals' your Mother
About the same wedding
For which you chose the venue.

"Aren't you two years
Older than her?
Or is it three
Yéwandé tell me?"

"What about that boy
That was always here?
The tall one that drives a red car.
Have you shown him the red card too?"

You already know
How these 'sessions' go.
You do not say a word,
It's always without worth.

--

The day ends.
You lay on your bed

Cursing *Bellanaija*‡ under your breath.
Till there is a sudden silence
And a calm voice saying—
"Daughter relax, let your hair down.
The world will never run out of Saturdays".

ANOTHER DAY

Every morning
Like a book
The clouds open.

Blurry moments pass
Then the sudden end
Of what was a start.

And

It makes me wonder why
Time never waits,
He does not wane
He takes no break
Not even for a little while.

EVEN TIME

No one rushes Love
Till she is ripe,
Not even Time—
She arrives

When she likes.

WHO WILL WARN IREPELOLA

The pleasures of a journey
The beauty of any new journey
By boat, by road or by the aisle
Is in how it pre-tickles your imagination.

Your heart lurches in expectation
Eagerly awaiting the known unknown
Your eyes twitch in anticipation
Of new sights soon to unfold
Your legs trip over your head
To approaching adventure drums.

But who will warn *Ìrépélolá*?
She has yet begun this journey
But we know she won't enjoy it
Her clothes kill imagination
And her husband has nothing
To look forward to at all.

WHAT A CHILD WANTS

It is never hard to figure out
What a child wants.
Perhaps it's the easiest thing in the world.
If he needed to pee
It would be transparently screamed.
If you needed to buy him a gift
Or wished to know what he wants to eat
You would not need a diagnosis kit—

Before you even speak, he would tell you;
"Daddy! Can we visit the zoo?" Or
"Mummy! I want a real car this time
One with blue tyres and a loud horn"
Or "Grandpa, I want a gun
Like the one in the movies
One that doesn't shoot water".

The requests might be silly
Or make you scream, but
In plain consistency, and
Unequivocal words
A child would tell you what he wants.
Not with silence, not with signs
Not with body murmur

Not with paradoxical outcries
Not with obscured *hint-entions*
But with precisely simple and
'Crystally' clear expressions.

I wonder at what point along the way
Children that have become wee-men
Lost this incredible gift?

A POT OF MUD

Last night the boy was thirteen
This morning he is thirty
To look out of his window
Asking 'where did the days go?'
Like pages of an open book
Turned by the wind.

But that is truth and that is life
To sleep a child and wake a man
And your memory of all between
As clear as a pot of mud
While you are ready
Like a clown on the battleground.

THE GAP

Your smile reveals a fence of ivory
Guarding that gap into heavenly bliss
I really don't care
If you smile at me or not
I only want you to smile.

So smile, reveal that bridge
Dividing dreams and reality
You know I don't care
If your smile is mine or not
Just smile. It's all I want.

TODAY I LIVED

Today I escaped
From the prison
Of my computer screen.

Today I went wild
In a vast and open field,
A place where smooth stones,
Grasses, shrubs and trees live.

Today I ran without a mark
And I danced like a fool.

Today I threw stones at the sun
And I farted into the winds.

Today, I had no care at all
Today I was free
Today I lived.

INSTAGRAM§

The muscles in your mouth
Have frozen in a permanent
Duckface!
And if your face had a mouth
It would complain
Since you have dyed her life out
To make 10,000 strangers
Fall in;
Lust—
With your body.

Your lips drip with honey
But you are still hungry.
You thought their words
Would warm you up
But they didn't do plenty
For your *empty-mess*—
You only burn for more.

Would you know before it's late?
The body is a savage.
If it feeds (on attention)

§ 'Instagram' is an online photo-sharing social media platform.

Before the spirit has had a fill
The spirit starves—
Slowly.
And while your body lives
Your spirit grieves.

Would you hear her screams?
Or would the noise
Of virtual strangers
Drown her out?

MIS-GUIDED

Affections will swiftly turn
The most nonchalant individual
Into a psychotic, pedantic analyst
Dissecting words and whispers
And silences and muffled breaths,
And loud cackles and low laughter
And smiles and misplaced glances
And perceived lingering gazes.
Extracting ridiculous premises
From a mere 'hello'
Or revealing profound meanings
Between the wings of dead flies.

While the heart seeks
Signs and metaphors,
The head says
"Calm down silly
It's just a dead fly".

But how can you hear your head
When your heart is faraway?

HAIR BUSINESS

I smile at you
Yours lights the room.

You run your fingers through 'your' hair
But then I want to run from here.

I see you, and I see visions
Of a bald and pissed Brazilian girl.

BAD DECISIONS

As thunder drowned the 9pm news
Mother picked her letters
The postboy left hours earlier.
Ralia slinked out through the kitchen
Dressed in strings and an umbrella.

Mother called, "Ralia my daughter
Please don't do tonight
What you'll regret in the morning"
She cocked her head and replied
"Thoughtless decisions, Mother
Make the most interesting stories".

And she was right in every bit
We were there, weren't we?
As the clergyman told it
At her hurried funeral.

But just a day after
The postboy still brought letters
And three or four weeks later
Her mother still sold cakes
By the Anglican school gates.

EPITAPH

Here lies *Òjó Ayékòótó*
Husband to one, Father of four.

He did not see the world
He had no time for fun.

He did not start a fire
He did not quench one either.

Note-worthy or exciting
He did nothing at all
Save eight hours daily
For thirty-two years
At the department of works.

FLOWN (For Tóní)

This morning I woke up
And didn't pull your hair
With those teasing words
I say every time.
I couldn't since I woke up
Next to an empty room,
Void, except for a bed
That mockingly yawns
With the hollow of when
You last slept in it.

This afternoon, I went to church
And everyone was
Glad to inform me
With news they heard from me.

"Now she's gone, how do you feel?"

So I smiled at them on the outside
But gave them head knocks in my head.

This night is the end
Of the first day you left
But clichés hate the mouth

Of this brooding poet
Though I often wonder
What's the point of it at all
To say the simple things
But complicatedly
Such as "I miss you"
Or "I love you".

I'm certain however,
You'll enjoy your new bed
While I watch things
Scatter together here.

*For my sister, with whom I shared a London flat
for 3 years, before she 'ran away' to America
with a man who gave her a wedding ring.*

SHAMELESS

Rotten grass is food
To a starving man,
(He'll even steal to survive) as
A rioting belly knows no shame, (and)
An 'un-food-filled' one, fears no rebuke.

A woman in labour has no regard
For protocols, funerals or solemn rites.
She'd scream for help and wouldn't care
If the physician was busy
Making children with his wife.

Like this dying man scrambles for air
Scribbling dire words with his blood.
He wants to live, (so) he wants you now.

ABRACADABRA

It's bedtime on a clear night
And my bedroom blinds are raised high
Enticing strings of silvery moonlight
That saunter in through conniving windows.

The feeling it brings, though beautiful
Isn't the best in the world
Neither is falling in love, nor
Being loved by another.

Tell me, what feeling can beat
The magical relief a woman feels
Finally reaching home from a bustling day
To care-freely release from their linen jails
The grateful captives of abracadabra?

PARTING WORDS

"Listen my son", Father asked.
Ségun squeezed tight Father's hand.

If you find someone
To grow old with
You will never grow old.

If you find a cause to live for
You will never die.

He said these words
And eased his hold
As cries of sorrow
Shredded the dawn.

I LAUGH AT
THESE SKINNY GIRLS

Have you seen these
Skinny things with glossy skin
That live near the cinema
With their chopstick necks
And matchstick limbs?

I hear they call me
"The bald old woman
That smells of cinnamon
With her rusty slow feet
And hanging dry tits".

I laugh.

Listen, silly girls
With your rainforest heads
Toothpick waists
And canopy chests
Whatever goes up
Surely comes down
And I can only laugh
At what time will confirm.

ÀDÙKÉ

Àdùké the daughter of *Ìwàlewà*
I heard your bargain-loving husband
Was yet to set his eyes on you
When you already caught his eyes
Hawking your very cheap wares.
He was yet to even hear you speak
When your discounts reeled him in.

Very well played *Àdùké*, well done.
Keep him out of the market however,
The sellers there have huger stalls
That are open in every weather
They are in hundreds or even more
And their wares are ten times cheaper.

PERSPECTIVES

Of what use is a royal cruse
And a wide crack spanning it?
The sun is fiery, the sun is hot
But it's not the stars you need
If your clothes are dripping streams.

Of what use is running fast
Towards a lion ending a fast¶?
If death is sure tomorrow,
Does it matter to curse the king?

A hole is beautiful
With a gold earring in it
But not to a man with holes
From the woman he swore he knows
One in his pocket, one in his heart.

¶ A period of abstaining from food.

A TICK AT A TIME

The sun yawns another day off
And I keep thinking I have time
But time keeps having me
A tick at a time.

MADIBA *(For Nelson Mandela)*

We have heard
The sad tales
Of the tale-teller
Of how the last-breath thief
Prevailed over *Mandela*.

But he must tell
Of how, in silencing him, he failed
For his deeds will still
Ink the faces of books
And the simple and the sages
Won't cease to hail
How he lived
And for what he stood.

STUBBORN STONES

At a time no one knew who *Facebook* was
And with oily mouths fenced with crumbs
And pockets pregnant with gritty stones
Borrowed from building sites nearby
We would run to puddles and ponds
Just to laugh at ripples after the plop.

At a time curly cords came with bulky phones
On familiar streets we would merry-go
Chasing chickens with tyres from old *Peugeots*
We would settle for low-hanging mangoes
When we failed to persuade our stones
To knock down ripe high ones mocking us.

Now we're grown, but who would have known
That unripe mangoes earned with bruises
(And sweat and stubborn stones and misses
And climbs and crawls and broken fences
In school uniforms with bubbly accomplices)
Taste sweeter than ones bought from chain
stores.

Part Two

I WILL SHOW YOU (PEPPER)

This morning, *Tade's* father fell
Into the pond near the barber's shop.
He was pulled out unharmed
But dripping with shame
Since everyone knew why he fell in,
Staring at your hips
While you passed innocently.

The fence around your mother's house
Is falling down as well, under the weight
Of the throngs of boys and men
From your street
(And the other streets) who lean on it.
They come each morning
Like antelopes to the waterhole
Thirsty to gulp a glimpse of you
They still saw the day before.

Daily, one by one, marinated in your awe
They come, with offerings of names.
They call you the nemesis of the moon,
And the eyes that bully the sun at noon,
They call you the heat-on-butter smile
They call you the purr of the evening breeze,

They call you the skin of glass to the eyes
And the skin of silk to the feel.

They call you names
As you inspire them like wine
But the only answer they get
Is the language of your ivory legs,
The flutter in your supple cheeks,
The pout of your lips, the spell in your eyes
And the way it seems
Even the wind waits on you to speak.

Each morning, I watch from a distance,
As you chase them away with stones.
You say love is overrated?
Wait till I show you (pepper)**.

** In Nigerian parlance, if you 'show someone pepper', you punish them or prove your worth to them, could be used in a playfully vindictive manner. Example: "You think our team is rubbish? Today on the field, we will show you pepper".

DOUBLE BED

Like birds all friends
Have flown out of the nest
They have sought and they have found
Joyful harvests elsewhere
While I still return to hollow walls
In a house empty of a lover's warmth.

I return certain that everything
Would be as they were when I left
Till I wonder, will children's laughter
Ever echo through these rafters?
And how much longer will I wait
Before I need a double bed?

SURVIVAL

Rice and beans will keep alive
But there is food to be alive.

How do I tell her
Her eyes
Give me life?

If her smiles die
How shall I survive?

BUSY

Every corner of summer
Is littered
With hugs and kisses
And it seems
Everyone has found love
While I am busy
Pretending
I'm not searching.

MARRIED PEOPLE

They offend me
With their love
In summer,
Kissing on the streets.

In winter,
It's the *hint-ention* in his eyes
The *him-patience* in her hands
And their home-hurrying feet.

OPPORTUNITY COST

Come here.
Stop killing me
From a distance
My dear.

Come hear
The one thing
I yearn to tell
Your ears.

Than keep my distance
I would rather
Empty my lips at your feet.

It is a choice, an opportunity cost
To keep dignity
Or lose sanity
I would rather keep my sanity.

For of what use is dignity
To a man the mere
Batting of your eyes
Drive out of his mind?

TURN AROUND

You are my atlas.
He is your map.
I chase after you.
You chase after him.

I wonder
Who will first
Turn around?

Will he turn
To love you?

Will you turn
To give in?

Will I turn
To give up?

TELL ME

Tell me to stop
And I won't breathe
Tell me to come
And I will sprint—
I will sprint
Like my life depends on it.

I'm here
With limbs in waiting
And ears standing still.

But you don't
Tell me anything.

ADEBOLA

If a mirror gets broken
Into sixty different pieces
It becomes more potent
Seeing in fifty-nine more places
It becomes more dangerous
Each piece with points and sharp edges.

Adébólá you broke my heart
Into sixty different pieces
And with each of these heart pieces
I'm watching you closely
And with their points and sharp edges
I will cut into your skin.

BELLING THE CAT

She smiles like a lamp
There is a rumble in my chest
I bully my face to answer her smile.
The food is good
The music too
But who thinks of roasted meat
When your tongue is on the spit[††]?

There are three words
She has to hear.
Like a clumsy bag of oranges
I spill them—

The silence that follows
Is the awkwardness
Of two men
In a public toilet
Peeing 'side by size'.

[††] A slender pointed rod for holding meat over a fire.

HAPPILY BLIND

Don't you see me
Scaling your walls
Walking your storms
Jumping through hoops
And playing your fool?

Don't you see me
At all?

Am I busy
Erecting signs
For someone
Happily blind?

STUPID MEN

Though this is 'battle-ry'
They have no idea.
It's weapons we carry
And war paint we wear
But they see 'makeup-ry'
And beautiful hair
Till fury darts flurry
Their blood everywhere.

DELIRIOUS

The heart is deceitful
Above all things (or)
Why should it say
You'll be good for me
When I'm daily dunked
In your side-effects?

As you rob me of my mind
I rub hair cream on my skin
And I'm adding salt to tea.

Sometimes I sing to dead flies
Or call your name out in my sleep.

I did you to me (that's granted)
But why make my thinking slanted?

A CHOICE THAT CANNOT BE CHOSEN

To sigh and to wait
Is all that is left
To do and to say
When words have departed
From dried up lips
And limbs once with zeal
Have gone very weak.

Good intentions
Rarely make hate love,
Never made wrong right
And what's often left
Are choices; two, and simple;
To sink or to move on.

But too many books
And tales under the moon
(Or perhaps cutely folly)
Makes moving on
A choice
That cannot be chosen.

COLD WATER

Good intentions never
Pacified a grumbling belly.

Cold water does not
Douse an insult.

You know
What your lips mean
But I know
How your words feel.

WHAT GOES AROUND

What goes around
Comes around
Unless
It changes its mind.

And how can I
Give you anything
Unless
You open your hand?

TAXICAB

If you don't know
What you are searching for
You will find it
And have no clue at all
Is what she said to me,
With moist eyes and a made mind
That Saturday in September.

Oh did I shrug without a thought?
Watched her become a dot in my horizon?
Now it's 11 months like yesterday
But her tracks are cold, her taxicab long gone
And all things good have turned to soot.

And now, to wander around is all I want
Throwing stones at taxicabs
Like the one I paid to drive my joy away.

She was my time, but I let her fly
She was my world, but I built a wall and
Trapped myself on the unplastered side
Tortured by sounds without a sight.

STARVING

Through this strangled straw
Stop feeding me
Oliver Twist‡‡ portions
Of your attention
When your fountain can
Nourish a city
Yet you titrate for just so much
To keep me neither dead nor living.

Open the clouds of your heart my love.
Flood me.
Drown me.
Set me free.

‡‡ 'Oliver Twist', is the name of the main character in Charles Dickens' classic novel
also titled 'Oliver Twist'.

UNFAMILIAR GROUNDS

Where I once stood
Now I stumble.
Who won't tumble
On unfamiliar grounds?

The hunter stares
Down the darkness
Of his own barrel
And he sweats.

For once he knows
How the buffaloes felt.

SNAFU§§

Tonight, a smooth wide road
Turned into a deep dark hole
Behind a dirty lonely alley
Like a lump of fat on a red hot slab
Or a sugar cube in a watery cruse
Or a pack of tired cards,
A frigging falling pack of cards.

Tonight I am alone on the long walk home
Grating my teeth and biting my lips
Thinking of things I said to her;
Of the ones that came out wrong
Of the ones not said at all.

§§ Confusion or chaos regarded as the normal state. It is a U.S. military slang, which
originated around 1941. It's an acronym for 'situation normal, all fucked up', expressing
a soldier's acceptance of the disorder of war. It means 'the situation is bad, yet a normal
state of affairs'.

PLANS AND TIME

Mellow drums and jazzy strings
Lull this restaurant to sleep
Like flames calmed
By the daze of light seductive rain
But in my head is a pandemonium—
Two mad bulls, raging in a cabin of wood
Or a tree brought to its knees
By bellowing relentless winds.

I'm on the edge of my head
At this table for two
Taunted by the empty seat in my view
I've been here before
In the company of laughter
But this eerie air
Soggy with heaviness is unfamiliar
It's like whistling while frowning
Or talking to silence
Or dancing to the rushing sound
Of passing cars.

Through this smudgy glass
I see the fleeting street
Filled with impassioned eyes

And hurrying feet
They have plans, but have no time
I have time, but no plans in sight.

I've been here before
In the company of laughter
They were dripping
Freely from your lips
Like bountiful juices of grapes
With beautiful bruises laced
Till one day
I stepped out of my head
And now you're gone
Like midday dew.

You were my plan, and you left
But left me with idle time.

Of what use is time however
Without a plan, good company
And a fair weather?

WAITING FOR MONDAY

Many times I have looked
Out of this broken window hoping
Not to see the same things
Dusk fell upon the night before.
Ants are not (yet) antelopes, neither has
Yesterday stopped the next day's dawn.

FALLEN

Falling in a place I once stood firmly
And "I saw it coming"
Is a big fat lie.

When I'm often on the throwing end
Of these deadly projectiles.

Till roles were reversed and
Like a sieve, I'm riddled with holes.

So this is how it feels?

BAD NEWS

My phone rings
But it's bad news
A knock on my door
But it's bad news
It's all bad news
Until it's you.

RICKETY CRADLE

Perhaps this is love
Perhaps a chair of fog
Sooner than later
This rickety cradle
Will choose a side and fall
To the right or to the wrong.

GATHERING STONES

How time flies when you are busy
Ignoring its consistent ticking.
That pretty flower must know how it feels
Growing on a fence many people pass by
And yet not earning a glance.

I now stand at the shore
At the expense of my sight
Talking to the sun
As harsh waves crash into the winds
Mocking my voice and the beats in my
chest—
Please tell me, is this how you felt
When you gave me your attention
And I took it without even looking?

I was busy gathering stones, silly me
You were my time, but I let you fly
You ticked consistently, but busy me was
Gathering stones to build an ignorant wall.

Now I stand on your other side
And this stone wall has no peep crack.

PHOTO FRAMES

I went to the stores today
And bought a photo frame
I've hung it on my wall
Though it holds nothing at all.

So I went searching again
Like yester-years and yester-days
And till I find you I will search
Over hills and desert land.

And one day no longer far
I will hold you in my arms
You will grace the frames like art
Like you'll always frame my heart.

WHO IS SHE?

Who is she?
Who is she?
Who is she?
Who is she?
Who is she?
Who is she?
Who is she?
Who is she?
Who is she?
Who is she?
Who is she?
Who is she?
Who is she?
Who is she?
Who is she?
Who is she?
Who is she?
I'm bewitched?
How does she
From a distance
Do this to me?

SEAWATER LOVE

To have great love
Is not enough
For great love
Is like a seesaw
It is useless
Like seawater
Unless there's someone
Who will share.

Part Three

ONE DAY

One day,
Writers will write
Our story of love
In books
That'll become
The textbooks
For perfect love.

The young will read
And dream
Of beautiful things.
The old will re-find
How having said
And done it all
One thing alone stands—
It is love.

SYMBIOSIS

He is tall, she is cutely short
And as such, he loves her much.

They are the size of balance—

He keeps her on her toes
She keeps him on the ground.

FORESKINS

Words won't say enough
Of how it's only you I love
They justly won't describe
How for you my heart longs.

If we were in Bible Times,
I would say it with a drink
From the enemy's territory.
I would say it with foreskins
Of four hundred Philistines.

FIND AND SEEK

She thought she'd love
The most beautiful one
She laid her eyes upon,
But the one she found

Became—

The most beautiful one
She could ever want.

WASTING TIME

I stood on a balcony
Overlooking the station at Albany
Watching people pour out of a hole
Like a hill of disturbed termites.

I saw a troubled mother struggle
To sight her quick-footed rascal
Having fun darting through
The throng of hurrying bodies.

It reminded me of your pearly eyes;
My favourite place to hide
And be lost
And found
And lost again.

And found
and lost again
As there is no fulfilling way
To waste time
Except solving puzzles of your eyes.

BLANK STARES

You tie my tongue
In a hopeless twist
Which ties me up
In a helpless heap.

I wish to speak
But all I can say and do
Are lifeless stares and
Looney doodles
After times
You have stunned my mind
And enchanted my sight.

6:45 AM

Everyday
The morning wakes
And makes a sun.

You are my sun
And every morning
You wake
And make my day.

11:45 PM

As you read
The streets are lonely and
Honest people are inside.

As you read
My bed embraces me
As I embrace dreams
Of you.

EVERYTHING ELSE

Only the one who has inhaled
Love dust can report how
All at once, everything else
Means nothing at all at, that
Instant the one your heart leaps for
Dives into your eager arms as
Everything else ceases to be.

LOVE AND GEOGRAPHY

If they stood in a line
The seven billion people
In the world would go
Around the earth
Forty-four thousand
Two hundred and ninety times
Yet of all, you my love
Are my favourite.

REWRITING THE BIBLE

One day I will be morally enabled
To create all the risqué poetry
I have waited forever to write
And to you alone for the rest of my life.

Together we will rewrite significantly
A certain book of the bible.

WHITE RICE

There is the hunger of the belly
There is the hunger of the heart.

A saucer of stew and
A bowl of white rice
Cures the hunger of my belly.

A beam of your smile
And the look in your eyes
Cures the hunger of my heart.

FULL MOON

It's eight days and a year
Since I last saw you
And I'm wondering what
You are doing right now.

It's an unusual evening
Of spring, as
The skies of London
Are spattered with clouds
Embroidered in hues
Of purple, orange and blue
And it's hard to tell
If this is an impatient moon
Or it's the sunset that delays.

And I'm wondering what
You are doing right now.
Are you, as well
Watching this sunset?
Can you see those tiny planes
Slicing across that full moon?

STARS AND COCKLEBURS

If you have seen the midday sun
You have only seen her eyes
When their lids are down.

Every dusk—

Who do you imagine bullies the sun?

Her eyes stay on the mind
Like cockleburs
As your eyes have to wander through hers
Only once.

Her eyes are
Like stars
Wise men seek after—

I am a man
And oh
I am very wise.

HARD THINGS

The second hardest thing in the world
Is finding you.
Precious things
Are hard to find.

The hardest thing in the world
Is losing you.
To lose you
Is to lose my life.

These hard things make
The easiest thing in the world
Loving you.

Till we have lost our hair
And everything that goes up
Has stayed down.

About the Writer

About the Title

ABOUT THE WRITER

Tolu' Akinyemi is an Architect, Entrepreneur, and a passionate Creativist. He was born in Akure, the sleepy capital city of Ondo State, Nigeria. He currently lives in London, England.

You can find Tolu on Instagram and Twitter (@poetolu). He blogs at poetolu.com/blog.

'I Laugh at These Skinny Girls' is his second published work. Watch out for new books on the way; *'To Cook A Stone' (Poetry)*, *'Bobolaya The Land of Liars' (folktale)* and *'These Bus Has Room for Forty People' (An illustrated and very cheesy little book for people in love).*

ABOUT THE TITLE

It was a summer evening in Woolwich, a diverse community in the south-east part of London, England. I was walking on the very narrow pavement of a street called 'Artillery Place', and ahead of me was a group of three or four chatty and attractive young women, in the prime of womanhood. They must have been in their early twenties.

Ahead of them was an elderly lady who looked seventy in the least, trudging along with a pace and demeanour typical of most people her age. It was a fairly long stretch of narrow pavement around a curved part of the road, bounded on one side by a stone wall, and on the other by vehicular traffic.

The old lady had everyone behind her moving at a very slow pace, and the obvious way to get ahead of her was to step off the narrow pavement into the busy road. The alternative was to continue at the slow pace till the end of the narrow stretch where the pavement widened.

I found the situation amusing, but the

young ladies didn't. They got impatient, and rudely made the old lady aware of this.

The poem '*I laugh at these skinny girls*' which is also the title of this book, recaptures from a comical perspective what I consider might be a justified retort from the old woman, towards the rude young women, who tried to bully her.

It also hopes to draw attention to ageism issues, and the declining respect and decorum young people have for, and around the elderly in a lot of modern societies.

"The glory of the young is their strength: the beauty of the old is their gray hair."

-King Solomon

(Proverbs 20:29)